T0381001

EMILY

THE WARRIOR

BILL KENNEY

authorHOUSE

AuthorHouse™
1663 Liberty Drive
Bloomington, IN 47403
www.authorhouse.com
Phone: 833-262-8899

This is a work of fiction. All of the characters, names, incidents, organizations, and dialogue in this novel are either the products of the author's imagination or are used fictitiously.

Published by AuthorHouse 11/15/2023

ISBN: 979-8-8230-1703-9 (sc)
ISBN: 979-8-8230-1704-6 (e)

Library of Congress Control Number: 2023920864

Print information available on the last page.

Any people depicted in stock imagery provided by Getty Images are models, and such images are being used for illustrative purposes only.
Certain stock imagery © Getty Images.

This book is printed on acid-free paper.

DEDICATION .

To my children, grandchildren, and all the others who put their hearts and sweat into their sport.

CHAPTER ONE

Emily Barker slunk to last chair on the team bench and buried her face in her hands. Her cheeks burned and the tears failed to cool them as she let her almost six foot tall, skinny body sag into the chair, one of twelve squeezed into the narrow space between the sideline of the basketball court and the cream-painted cement block wall of the small gym in her middle school.

Fouling out of this critical game was unforgivable. This was the semi-finals of the Morris County; NJ eighth grade tournament and her Ridge Middle School team was losing to Forsythe by two points with only two minutes left. And they had beaten Forsythe by 20 points only two weeks ago.

To make matters even worse, her father was standing up in front of the two rows of bleacher seats on the opposite side of the court berating the pudgy, gray-haired man in the striped shirt who had just called the foul that forced her to the bench. Emily got her height from her father who was 6'2" and broad-shouldered. Though his black hair was flecked with gray, his face was as red as a petulant child's as he shouted across the court.

"You're blind, You should have retired years ago. You let that fat kid push our girls around the whole game and then you call a touch foul on our best player. You're cheating our kids!"

The offending referee was standing near the scorer's table directly across the court from John Barker, who was standing right at mid-court. He was the only spectator in a charcoal gray business suit and the only one saying anything. The other 20 or so just sat in shocked silence, or perhaps private glee at the loss of Ridge's star player. In this gym her father's voice was as loud as the roars in Madison Square Garden.

Her father's tirade only made matters worse for Emily. She buried her face in a towel and covered her ears with it.

Just then the other referee ran up to the Ridge coach, Brian Costello, his face contorted in anger.

"Where's your athletic director?" he shouted.

"He's not here today," answered the coach.

"Well then you get to do the job. I want that clown out of here!"

The coach took the referee by the arm and led him away from Emily so she could not hear.

"That's the father of the girl who just fouled out. She's huddled at the end of the bench crying. Do we have to make it worse for her?"

"Yeah? Well, her father is yelling at my father. He goes or the game is over!"

Costello opened his mouth as if to argue, but then thought the better of it, sighed and walked across the court to Mr. Barker. The place fell silent.

"Mr. Barker," he said quietly, "you have to leave, or the referee is going to forfeit the game to Forsythe."

"They can't do that."

"I'm afraid they can. Please go."

"It's snowing out."

"I'm sure you have your car here."

Slowly Emily's father picked up his topcoat and put it on. Just as slowly he walked to the exit with his head up and left. A blast of cold air signaled his departure, and the funeral-like silence was broken by a Forsythe fan that started to applaud. She was quickly followed by others.

The noise caused Emily to lift her head just as her father reached the door. When she realized what was happening, she burst into tears, her mind exploding: *Oh God no! It's the end of my world.* Once more she buried her face in the towel.

The day that had started with so much promise had turned miserable early on. She was used to scoring 20 points and getting 11 rebounds a game but could manage only 10 points today. Forsythe had double-teamed her for the whole game with a shorter, but very husky, girl behind her to keep her away from the basket and a quick guard in front to keep the ball away from her. She had suffered through a lot of bumps throughout the season, some of which were hard enough to cause her to fall. She had trained herself to jump right up. Today the referees never seemed to notice what caused her to go down. Ridge was losing, and she was convinced it was her fault.

Her coach had said nothing to her as she had come off the court. She could feel his disappointment, and that of the silent substitutes and fans.

Worse yet, Suzy Highland and Courtney Ambrose, who were sitting directly across the small gym from her with classmates Ralph Steele, Billy Pedrazi, and Bobby Martin, were looking at her and laughing. *They're probably making jokes about her father,* she was convinced.

She was roused from her funk by an elbow in the ribs.

"Coach wants you to sit next to him," said Joan, a little girl who rarely got in a game and always sat at the far end of the bench.

Emily was tempted to ignore the message, but a second poke in the ribs was reinforced by a shout from the coach.

"Big E get over here. You know I can't leave the coaching box."

"Big E" was a nickname that she hated all the time, but today it was especially painful. Emily was sure she was watching the end of her season and the failure of all the effort she had put in during the previous spring and summer to improve her game.

Yes, she was tall at 5'-10", but literally, skinny. She weighed perhaps 120 after Thanksgiving dinner. Her arms and legs looked as if any bump would crack them in two, perhaps in contrast to her broad shoulders and big feet, both of which signaled future growth.

She had played soccer also through fifth grade and was a pretty good goalie. When she got to middle school, both basketball and soccer became year long activities. Between the school teams, travel teams and AAU basketball teams, all with coaches demanding priority, there were too many conflicts for her and her family to deal with. She had enjoyed the sunny spring soccer games but hated freezing her skinny tail off in some Thanksgiving weekend tournament. She chose basketball for some inner, perhaps genetic reason, or maybe because of the bored look on her father's face when he watched her soccer games.

Her father, who had been a sub on the Manhattan College basketball team 20 years ago, encouraged her to play as much as she could. She did that, was sought after last spring by the AAU 14U team in the area, even though she was a year younger than most of the players on the team. She was picked for the Morris County all-star team which got to the final four of the State tournament.

There were prices to pay for this success and attention. Her father came to many of her games even though he worked in New York City, bearing a brief case full of work papers that had to be dealt with after supper. He was her biggest fan, but sometimes she wished he'd be quieter at her games and talk to her about something else besides basketball. Then there were

Suzy and Courtney, who spent the summer socializing with the boys at the town pool while Emily sweated in places like the Newark YMCA and the Queens College Athletic Center. A lot of those games also conflicted with her singing in the church choir on Sunday mornings, something she missed more than the sermons.

And then there were the social costs, which at this critical moment suddenly seemed important. Emily's brown hair was flat and short enough to tuck behind her ears because it was easier to deal with on the court. She had to admit that the other girls' hair looked better. It was longer and still had a few blonde highlights from the summer sun. Her experience against the bigger girls last summer had toughened her to the point where she felt comfortable playing ball with Ralph, Billy, and some of the other boys in her class. However, she wasn't at all sure that the boys even thought of her as a girl despite their time together. And now it seemed that even her athletic ability had gone down the tubes.

She was sure the coach was about to rub salt in her wounds. Her eyes overflowed again, but she got up and shuffled toward him.

Coach Costello, a retired teacher who used to coach the boys' team at the regional high school, slapped his hand on the chair to his right. He had volunteered to coach the girls' team at Ridge School when it started six years ago, and was still at it, working hard every day for the joy of seeing his charges learn the game and improve their skills. Emily sat, keeping her eyes on the gym floor.

"I'm sorry, coach," she said, rushing the words out between sobs. "I stunk today."

"It's OK, Emily. It's OK. You can't do it all every day. Right now, I need you to help me. Watch how they play Sally while I try to adjust the offense."

Sally Glass was the girl who substituted for Emily. She was almost as tall as Emily and even skinnier. She was a semi-coordinated seventh grader, an inadequate substitute who got to play only after games were decided.

Dutifully, Emily watched as both teams lined up for the free throws resulting from her foul, but she was having trouble concentrating. *How could she have stunk up the place so badly today?*

The Forsythe girl who lined up next to Sally was two inches shorter, but twice as wide and very strong. Next to Sally she looked like a grown woman.

The gym got silent as the Forsythe player prepared to take the first shot of a bonus penalty which could result in Forsythe's leading by four points.

The shot hit the side of the rim and bounced away. The home crowd roared, but the stocky girl next to Sally got the rebound, and Sally fell as she turned to guard her. The girl made the lay-up to give Frosythe a four-point lead anyway. Emily hung her head again.

Once more she got an elbow in the ribs. This time from Coach Costello.

"Watch how they play Sally."

After a moment or two it became clear that they weren't going to play Sally at all. Ridge's only remaining offensive threat was Caitlin Arbour, their point guard, and a good dribbler. Forsythe's big girl ignored Sally and just stood in the middle of the lane to prevent Caitlin from dribbling to the basket. Caitlin stopped just inside the foul line and sank a jump shot before the big girl could reach her. Ridge was losing now by only two points. Forsythe called time out.

When play resumed, Forsythe went into a stall offense. With one- and one-half minutes left their guards dribbled and passed the ball out near half court, while the Ridge guards chased them around. Every time that Ridge got one of the guards in a little trouble, she passed to the big wide girl at the top of the key. Sally could not seem to get in front of the girl in time to prevent the pass.

"Front her! Front her, Sally," yelled Emily, but Sally just wasn't quick enough to get around the wide body in time.

Finally, one of the Forsythe guards fumbled the ball and Caitlin jumped on it. She immediately asked for time out right from the floor. There were 25 seconds left in the game.

As the team gathered Emily grabbed Coach Costello's arm.

"Coach, after practice most days Sally stays and tries three-point shots. She's gotten pretty good at it. They aren't playing her at all, so why not let her try one?"

The coach took a look at Sally, who was standing at the fringe of the circle of players and looking at the floor. He got the impression that the heat of any responsibility would cause her to melt completely.

"At the moment, I doubt if she could reach the basket," he said, almost to himself.

Emily grabbed Sally.

"Sally, tell coach how you've been sinking three-pointers after practice."

The crestfallen Sally said, "Gee coach, I don't know. I've never shot one in a game."

Coach thought a moment. Then he said, "Let's run that pick play for Caitlin's jumper again, and everybody crash the boards!"

Emily sighed and slumped back into her chair.

Caitlin took the ball for the throw-in and quickly threw it to a mysteriously wide-open teammate. The girl tried to throw it back to Caitlin but found her double-teamed. Forsythe was going to prevent Ridge's only remaining scorer from even getting the ball!

As Ridge struggled to get the ball to Caitlin, the clock ticked on: 15 seconds . . . 10 seconds. . . .

Suddenly Coach Costello shouted, "Throw it to Sally!"

Sally was standing at the head of the foul circle looking helpless. With three guards now around Caitlin it was easy to throw Sally the ball . . . 5 seconds. . .

"Shoot!" yelled the coach and Emily in unison.

Almost by reflex, Sally turned and shot.

"Yikes!" screamed Sally's mother.

The game-ending horn sounded, and the gym got quiet. It was as if everybody was holding his or her breath and the world was turning in slow motion. Every eye in the building was on the flight of the ball.

The ball hit the backboard, then hit the front rim and bounced two feet straight up.

Then the ball fell through the basket. The referee signaled three points.

Ridge had won!

All the players and substitutes jumped on a giggling Sally at the foul circle, but Coach Costello hung back, grabbed both of Emily's hands, and spoke quietly.

"I'd give you a big hug if I could. Despite your personal pain, you helped us win just as if you scored 30 points. There are going to be more bad days in your life, Emily. You'll have to learn to live with them. A few tears don't matter. If you don't ever give up, good things will happen."

-- -- -- -- -- --

It was fifteen minutes before Emily got to her father sitting in his car with the dome light on reading some business papers with the motor running and the heater blasting. There was the faint smell of gasoline in the passenger compartment. She slid into the passenger seat; her winter jacket zipped over her sweaty basketball uniform.

"What took so long?"

"We won the game, Dad. Caitlin hit a jumper and then Sally stuck a three and we won by one at the buzzer."

"Sally, that skinny seventh grader won the game for you?" asked her father. "Well, I'll be."

"Yep. It was awesome. It took a while for me to hug all the other players, even the ones who didn't play. This was the first day that I wasn't the star. I cried. They picked me up. They carried me. Now I really know what Coach Costello means when he talks about what a team is. I was so grateful to them and to him."

Her father grunted, then asked, "When is the tournament final?"

"Saturday."

"Before then I want to talk to your principal. What's his name again, Peters? I need to give him a piece of my mind about getting asked to leave the gym today."

Emily's face blanched. She almost shouted, "Please don't do that. Besides, they might ban you from the finals."

"What? They can't do that."

"They did today. I may have to learn to live with a bad game once in a while, even if I cry a little. That's bad enough, but having you get run out of the gym is way too uncool. I can't deal with that, especially in front of my friends."

"It doesn't matter what those socialites think."

Emily grabbed her father's arm. "They matter to me, Dad. They're my friends. Even though they're more social, they come to my games because of that. You have to promise me not to say one word at my games anymore. Not one word."

"You want me to make believe I'm one of those cool parents?"

"Dad, everybody knows you're intense. Acting cool wouldn't fool anybody for a minute. You just need to figure out how to be quiet: no yelling at the refs; no coaching; no nothing."

"So, you're giving me orders now?"

"Daddy, I need you to promise."

John Barker looked at his daughter. Her blue eyes bored into his. For the first time he realized that those eyes were the same as her mother's. For the first time her gaze didn't falter under his. "I'll do my best," he said, put the car in gear, and drove them back to the conventional split-level house Emily and her parents called home.

CHAPTER TWO

The Barker home sat on a deep lot with a great backyard on a side street off the main north/south road. Part of the backyard, of course, was devoted to a paved area featuring a basketball hoop. Until the 1950s the town had been very rural. There was a 1000 acre private estate, two farms and several greenhouse complexes. Then the estate was sold, part used to create the Morris County campus of an urban university, the remainder for the building of an engineering center for a major oil company. One of the farms and the greenhouses soon became housing developments, but one farm remains which hosts a dozen small, brown cows with thick menacing horns. The ancient red schoolhouse is maintained as a museum at the cross of main roads in the center of town, surrounded by banks, restaurants, a couple of chain drug stores and, of course, a Starbucks and a MacDonalds.

Emily lived close enough to walk to her school. The day after the game she arrived a few minutes early as she normally did, dressed in her down jacket, and knit hat, and carrying a green backpack stuffed with books, a sandwich, and clean gym clothes.

She found out very quickly that this was not to be a normal day. The story of her father getting thrown out of the gym had gone viral. She had to deal with the wise guys who teased her about it, and with the sympathy of her friends. Both caused embarrassment. Things got worse when she met the principal, Mr. Peters, in the hall and he asked for her father's work telephone number.

"I don't know it," she answered.

"I was going to call your mother for it, but since I ran into you, I thought you might save me that step," he explained.

"Why do you want to talk to him?"

The principal looked away for a moment then said, "Emily, you're a smart girl. We can't have our parents being asked to leave the gym at our games."

Emily pleaded, "I've talked to my father and have his word that there'll be no more trouble."

"His word?"

"His promise."

Mr. Peters was no taller than Emily. He looked her in the eye for a long moment before responding. "Very well, Emily. I'll trust you on that. Let's hope that the Eagle doesn't report the incident in this week's edition." That said he moved on toward his office.

Emily was filled with dread. She had never thought that the local newspaper would report her father's ejection, even though it normally did report the game scores. *God! Could anything else go wrong today?* She couldn't wait for classes to be over and get back out on the basketball court where things were simple.

- - - - - -

Coach had seen his counterpart from their opponent in the final, Central Middle School, scouting at the semifinal game. She was a wise young lady who had played in college. He knew that Emily would be double-teamed throughout the championship game and that Ridge would need a new strategy if they were to win the trophy.

At practice he worked on a new offensive system with Emily up at the foul line and passing the ball to the sides to Caitlin, and possibly Sally, for open shots. If Central's big girls came out on Emily at the foul line, then a teammate should be open at the basket for a quick pass from the Big E. If the defense did not rush to guard Emily, she could take what amounted to a foul shot, at which she was very good. This strategy would result in fewer shots for his star, but she might make up the difference by "crashing the boards" when someone else took a shot.

Coach Costello explained all this to the team, then he had them practice against his subs and some players from the boys' team whom he had recruited to provide a more realistic defense. Billy Pedrazi, who was almost 6'2", was assigned to guard Emily. Emily and the girls got the hang of the new system rapidly. The Big E also found that she got some good angles at the rebounds from her teammates' missed shots by starting from her position in the center of the foul lane. She also found herself on the floor more often, but she was filled with hope.

━ ━ ━ ━ ━ ━ ━

The final game was being played at the Foster School in Morris Township. The court was the biggest in the middle school league and provided five times as many seats for spectators as did the Ridge School gym. The stands were almost full before the game started, which filled the girls with awe. Never had so many people showed up to watch one of their games.

Emily's father, John, and mother Janet came early and claimed seats in the first row of the bleachers. Having her father so close to the court made Emily nervous.

She broke off from the warm-up drills for a moment of conversation.

"Dad there is always a parade of students walking back and forth to the snack bar and rest rooms during the game. You and mom would have a better view of the game if you moved up a couple of rows."

Her dad replied, "I can see over any kids walking." He stayed where he was, but Emily's mother moved up one row to sit directly behind John.

At least that's better, thought Emily. *Her mother could grab him if he forgot his promise and jumped up.*

Janet was three inches shorter than Emily and built a little more on the solid side of trim than the lean. She went to exercise class twice a week but was not a fanatic about it. Emily knew her mother was more than strong enough both physically and philosophically to exert restraint on her husband but was a little worried that she could react quickly enough.

Then Emily saw Mr. Peters arrive and greet her parents. He took a seat next to her father. She felt confident now that there would be no incidents at this game and focused on her warm-ups.

Central had two players almost as tall as Emily. They took turns guarding her from behind while one of their smaller players harassed her from the front when she got the ball. As planned, that left Caitlin, or another teammate open on one side or the other. Emily passed the ball quickly to the open girl. Things went well as the open girls made many of the shots, they had been practicing for the last three days.

Central quickly adjusted their defense, bringing the other big girl out from her position near the basket to contest the shots from the side. This left space near the hoop for a Ridge girl to step into. Emily faked a pass to the side and then whipped the ball to the girl underneath. After several easy baskets from there, Emily's guard dropped off to cover the open space. The Big E began to show her shooting skills from just inside the foul line. Coach Costello's system worked just fine. Ridge was ahead by fifteen points at half time.

The saying about the best laid plans of mice and men proved to be true in the second half: the shots stopped falling; Emily picked up two fouls rebounding; and Central began double-teaming Ridge's guards to make it much more difficult to pass the ball to Emily. On the other hand, that meant that Central's big girls were playing The Big E one-on-one, and when she did get the ball there was no stopping her.

Ridge won the championship game by ten points. Her father was standing in front of his seat, his fist pumping. Her school principal was standing next to him, clapping, and smiling.

After all the high-fiving and hugging was over and the trophy safely in hand, John brought a young woman over to talk to Emily. She had skin the color of milk chocolate and was dressed in designer jeans and high heels.

"This is Natasha Booker," he said. "She's the coach of the AAU 16U team based in Morristown that won the state championship last summer. She's also the assistant coach of the Morris Brown Prep team." His face was still a little flushed from the game, or maybe it was the attention of such a coach.

The woman said, "You had a fine game today, Emily. I was impressed with your knowledge of the game as well as your skill."

This was just icing on Emily's cake. She said, "Thank you," with a big smile, and maybe a little blush colored her fair cheeks.

"From what your father said you would still be eligible to play at the 14U level this summer, but I'd like you to try out for our 16U team. If you make the team, you'll learn a lot, and we have some nice trips planned for the summer. We're scheduled to play in a big weekend tournament in Pittsburgh."

It had been a long time since Emily had had to try out of any team. Her ego rankled at the thought but was impressed with the sophistication of the coach.

"When would this tryout be?" she asked.

"March first at the Morris Brown main gym at four."

"Wow, that's next week. How many girls will be there?"

"About a dozen, we have six or seven spots open on the team."

Emily looked at her dad. He was smiling and nodding his head.

Emily said, "OK, I'll be there. Thanks for the invite."

The coach smiled. "Great," she said. "You'll find that you are not going to be the biggest girl there. You'll have to learn some ways to deal with those bigger rebounders and not get any silly fouls. You'll also learn some things to improve your all-around game, because others will be playing at the five spot. Should help you a lot in your high school career."

The coach offered her hand, Emily shook it, and said "Look forward to all that."

The coach left and Emily's father could hardly wait for her to get out of earshot before exclaiming, "This will not only help your game, but also give you a shot at a scholarship to Morris Brown."

"Dad, please calm down. I haven't made the team yet and I'm not really interested in going to some fancy prep school. Let's just take one step at a time like you always say."

"Yeah, yeah, but this is a big deal."

Janet, Emily's mother, arrived just in time to hear that last phrase. "What's a big deal?"

Emily answered before her father because he was taking a deep breath in preparation for launching into an extended explanation. "I've been invited to try out for a 16U AAU team."

"You're not even 14 yet. Why would you want to bat heads with the bigger girls? You get knocked down often enough playing against girls your own age." said her mother.

"Yeah, but this would be a step up if I make the team. A good head start for the high school team."

"And maybe a chance at a scholarship to Morris Brown," interjected her father.

Janet looked at him and then spoke to Emily. "I thought you were going to limit the basketball a little this spring and summer. Have a more normal life."

Emily looked at the floor and then at her father, who had raised his brows in surprise. She said, "Yes, I want to do that, and I also want to play softball at school. Caitlin and Suzy play, and they say it's fun. No pressure. I liked playing Little League baseball."

"Whoa," said Dad. "16U will take a lot of time. That team won the state championship last summer."

"I know, Dad, but I could use a break. Let's just see if I make the team before we get all excited."

"Have you ever failed to make any team?" her father asked.

No, I haven't thought Emily, *but I have been looking forward to a more relaxing summer, fewer games, hanging out at the pool on teen nights, and maybe having some conversation with the boys that didn't have anything to do with basketball. Well, she wouldn't touch a ball for a couple of days.*

CHAPTER THREE

Emily's plans for a respite from basketball got over turned by Mother Nature. The sun was Spring-bright on Sunday; the wind was from the southwest, and the temperature climbed into the fifties after church. Her father insisted that she shoot some jump shots at the hoop in their back yard. "The practice will be good for your all-around game at the tryout," he said. Emily's heart wasn't in it, so she missed several, which prompted some instruction from her dad.

At last, her mother called from the back door. "Come on, brunch is ready."

"We need a few more minutes here," replied her father.

"The eggs will get cold."

Emily jumped into the conversation. "Come on, Dad. You know you hate cold eggs and so do I." She started for the door, still bouncing the basketball. Her father didn't move until the ball lay at the foot of the three steps up to the door and Emily was almost there. Her mom gave her a little hug as she entered the kitchen.

They ate at the round table in the breakfast nook off the kitchen. The original dining room had been converted into TV room/office because the family never held big sit-down dinner parties. Janet reached over Emily's head to put a bowl of scrambled eggs in the table. That done she grabbed both of Emily's shoulders and eased them into a fully upright position.

She said, "Always sit up straight, Ems. Be proud of your height."

"OK, Mom, OK, but I have to reach the eggs."

Janet just sighed.

Emily volunteered to help clean up the dishes from brunch in hopes that the big-time college basketball games on TV would claim her father's interest. She was right and seized the chance to escape to her text messages and Facebook page.

— — — — — —

The tryout was on Tuesday afternoon. Emily had not touched a basketball since Sunday and felt relaxed. Her mother drove her to the Morris Brown School and found a chair in the corner of an empty gym.

The gym itself was impressive. There were roll-up stands about ten rows high completely down one side of the court. The other side contained a long scorer's table and dozens of chairs for team players. The foul lanes were painted navy blue as were the boundary lines, and there was a huge space beyond the end lines at both ends of the court, rather than the three feet at the Ridge gym. There were dozens of other lines on the court, all in different colors. Green and navy -blue banners listing the various championships the school had won covered much of the wall above the team benches. To Janet it looked more like the gym at Manhattan College where she had met her husband.

The woman who would select the team, the same coach who had talked to Emily on Saturday, showed up dressed in an elegant warm up suit also in navy blue and dark green. Janet had to smile when she saw her shoes though. They were Converse low-cut sneakers similar to those worn by John at Manhattan 25 years ago, which were preserved as souvenirs in a box in their attic. Apparently, some things never go out of style.

Janet's first reaction was one of awe at the size of two of the dozen girls warming up. Not only were they at least three inches taller than Emily, but they also looked like they weighed a minimum of thirty or forty pounds more. *Perhaps there would more time to spend on things other than basketball during the warm weather,* she thought.

Her hopes did not recognize her daughter's competitive spirit. Emily was a step quicker than the bigger girls and, after a few minutes, figured out how to use that to her advantage. In a series of one-on-one drills Emily won as many contests as she lost. In three-on-three half-court games she used the extra space and her ability to coordinate with her temporary teammates to win each mini-game.

One of the bigger girls let her frustration get out of hand and slammed into Emily as she was shooting a layup. Emily went flying and almost crashed into the wall some ten feet behind the basket. Janet leaped out of her chair and started to sprint toward her daughter. She should have saved her energy. Emily jumped to her feet shouting her anger and punched the girl in the face.

The blow was more amazing to the girl than damaging. She backed up a step, raised both hands in a gesture of surrender, and said, "Easy there. I'm sorry. I got a carried away and hit you a little hard. Just couldn't let a skinny little white girl score on me again."

By this time the coach was between them and furious. She shouted, "If that had happened in a game you both would have been thrown out and we would probably lose. We can't tolerate that bush league stuff if we're going to repeat as state champions."

Emily's face was already red from anger, but redder still from the rebuke, and perhaps from the realization that if the big girl had retaliated, she might be heading for the hospital.

The big girl still held her hands in the air. "Got your message, coach. This ain't the school yard in the hood. I'll be cool from now on."

"Either that or you'll be back in the hood so fast your hair will straighten," snapped the coach. "Enough of this. Three of you at each basket for foul shots." She beckoned a smaller girl and took her over to a chair next to the scorer's table. After a few minutes of conversation, the girl picked up her backpack and sweats and left the gym. The procedure was repeated five more times until the only players left shooting foul shots were the two big girls, a lightning-fast little guard, two players from area high school JV teams, and Emily.

The coach blew her whistle and beckoned the group to come to where she sat. "OK you're it," she said. "Practice here at ten Saturday morning. The rest of our team will be here Saturday as well. Two of them may be dragging a bit because they're playing here Friday night in the finals of the Prep School League tournament. You're all welcome to come to that game. It would be a chance to see what kind of system we'll be playing this summer."

There were fist bumps all around. The girl who had knocked her to the floor held both hands in front of her face and faked fear with a big grin when Emily got to her. They laughed and bumped both fists. Next to Emily the girl was huge. Not only was she four inches taller, but she was also twice as wide. Her 180 pounds were distributed strategically over a big-boned, athletic frame, topped by a collection of short dreadlocks bleached blonde.

"My name is Maisia," the big girl said, "but that's too complicated for most players, so they call me Mo."

"I'm Emily."

"That's too complicated too. I christen you Bones."

Emily shrugged. "OK."

Mo shouted, "Hey guys meet Bones."

Everybody laughed, then began spitting out their own preferred labels, at least for basketball. "I'm Ronna," said the other big girl; "I'm Rene," shouted the water-bug guard. The two players with high school JV experience were Sarah and Jen, who had been playing against each other since the fourth grade.

Coach Booker waved her clipboard and said, "See you all on Saturday at ten. Don't be late."

Janet rose from her chair and sighed once more.

— — — — — — —

Emily's Dad insisted that they go to watch the game Friday night. Morris Brown was playing Gill St. Benedicts and was favored. The bleachers were almost full, but John found a seat in the front row as he usually did, and Emily climbed into one in the row just behind him.

The Morris Brown team consisted of a mixture of races. Half of the girls had skins in various shades of brown and black, and the rest were white. Coach Booker was there in her high heels, navy blue slacks and an elegant dark green blouse. The head coach was shorter than she, with flying white hair, baggy brown pants, and his tie askew. His suit jacket was already draped around the back of the chair nearest the scorer's table.

By contrast, the GSB team was lily white, though they matched up size-wise with their opponents quite well. Their coach was tall and looked as if he had been to championship games before. He wore a dark blue suit, white shirt, and red tie. His assistant was a tall woman who wore a red dress, and red high heels. The color matched the team uniforms

There were three officials assigned to this game, one of whom was female. They got through the preliminaries quickly and fist bumped the players with smiles during the introductions. They too, looked as if they had been involved with championship games before.

The Morris Brown starting lineup interested Emily. There were two black girls as big as Mo and Ronna from Tuesday's tryout. The only white player to start was one of the tri captains who participated in the pregame meetings. The GSB team had two players who were just as big as those from MB. Emily wondered where the big black girls on the MB team came from. They certainly had not been on any of the teams she played against in the three years she had been on the Ridge team in the Morris County eighth-grade league. Morris Brown must recruit in Newark or other cities.

It turned out to be a heck of a game. Morris Brown's big girls pitched every rebound they got out to speedy guards who raced down the court. Sometimes they threw the ball away, but often they got a layup. Their coach ran almost as much as the players did. He raced up and down in front of the bench depending on which end of the court the ball was at and grabbed substitutes off the chairs to enter the game seemingly at a whim, or maybe with divine inspiration. He never stopped waving his arms and shouting instructions and his shirt was soaked with sweat by the time the game was over. At that point, Coach Booker's elegant blouse had not a single wrinkle.

The GSB team ran the fast break when they could but played a more conservative offense. They passed the ball around a lot, often getting it to a high post player who passed it out to a shooter, just as Emily and the Ridge team had done the previous Saturday. The difference was that when GSB got a three-point shot against MB's pressing zone defense, they often made it. Their coach never took his suit jacket off.

The game reminded Emily of the tortoise and the hare story, but this time the hare won. MB had the substitutes to run incessantly for 32 minutes and wore the GSB team out by the time the fourth quarter came around.

Emily's father had been shouting his analysis of the play over his shoulder throughout the game, but with all the noise in the gym, Emily didn't capture much of what he said. She knew he would repeat it all on the ride home.

"What did you think?" he asked as they got into the car.

"They are awesome. They're all a lot bigger and faster than any team I've ever played with or against. On top of that, I thought the Morris Brown coach was going to have a heart attack before the game was over."

He father said, "I read where this is the fourth time his team has won the prep school championship in the last six years. His energy seems to get results."

"He must spend a lot of energy recruiting players too. Most of those girls didn't come from around here."

"I suspect coach Booker helps with that, but she comes from Summit, not some inner-city school. She played at Rider."

"You've been doing a lot of research, Dad. Please stay cool. It's six months before I get to high school."

"What does that mean?"

"Just a fact."

John got "Bones" to practice at 9:45 the next morning. The five girls who did not have to try out were already there. Two of them, one of the big black girls and the white captain from MB, had played in the championship game the night before. Their names were Tyree (Ty) and Joannah (Jo). Two others had seen some time on the Morris Catholic varsity which had won the Morris County tournament two weeks ago. They were twins: Ellen and Elaine who went by nicknames One and Two in order of their birth. The last of the players was one of the three-point shooters from the Gill St. Benedicts team named Kelly. Emily would have to work on those names later. At least the nicknames should be easy to remember. She was in awe at the array of talent on the court. She certainly would not be one of the "bigs" on this team, either in size or in experience.

Practice was a two-hour grind. There were drills to improve dribbling, passing, and shooting skills; three-person full court fast break drills at which dribbling was prohibited, and breakout sessions for the taller girls and the guards. Coach Booker took care of the training of the guards, while a big guy from the varsity boys' team led the session for the "bigs".

Emily was a "tweener". She was shuttled from one group to the other. She learned a lot about how to use her elbows discreetly and some fancy footwork during her time with the big girls, and that she was relatively slow compared to the smaller girls. She was convinced that her father would have her practicing all those things in her back yard tomorrow.

That night Emily's friends, Caitlin and Suzy, came over. They popped some corn and watched a movie on Emily's DVR. Both girls played on the Ridge softball team and wanted Emily to come out for the team.

"We need a good first baseman," Caitlin said.

"And the boys come out to cheer us on," said Suzy.

"It's been a long time since I played Little League baseball," replied Emily.

"So, what. It's just for fun," said Suzy.

Having some fun after all this serious basketball stuff sounded good to Emily. Practice was going to start next week. She'd have to make up her mind soon.

Chapter Four

Emily decided to try softball. After her stint as one of three girls playing baseball with the twelve-year-old boys in the town recreation league, she never graduated to the older girls' softball program. She found it easy enough to remember how to catch and throw the ball, but ground balls took some work. As the tallest girl on the team, she fell into the first base job without competition. And the boys did come out to cheer, and sometimes jeer, them on.

The weather was iffy during most of March. There were a several days when they didn't practice. It was definitely more laid back than Emily was used to on the basketball court. The first week of the season in April was rained out as well, so there were no conflicts with her AAU basketball activities, most of which were on weekends.

Their first softball game was at home against a team from Wharton. As the team was changing into their uniforms for the game, Emily got a big surprise: the eighth graders wore eye make up for the games. Suzy had on dark eye shadow and had done something to her eyelashes to make them look longer and blacker. Caitlin had a pastel shade over her eyes as well.

Caitlin saw Emily standing there with her mouth open, took her by the arm, and led her to a bench in a corner of the room. Their "team room" was a long cement block rectangle with a door at each end, really an over-sized rest room. It had benches along one wall, two toilet enclosures and two shower stalls on the opposite one, separated by a white board for instruction. Since none of the girls, even the sweaty basketball players, ever took a shower, one stall was filled with some netting and a five-gallon pail full of softballs. The other just sat there its grout dried out and cracking. The room smelled like a musty attic with hints of ammonia and bleach.

Caitlin told Emily, "Sit down. I'll fix you up Ems. If Suzy does it, you'll look like a Broadway actress."

"What is this business with the eye shadow," asked Emily.

"Years ago, some kid convinced her parents to allow an exception to the 'no make up until high school rule' for the team. We couldn't do that for the basketball team because the sweat would mess things up, but softball is cool, and the boys like it. A lot of the teams do it. Sit down; I'll take care of things for you."

She reached into her backpack and extracted a small case. In a few minutes she was done, took a step back to admire her work, and smiled in satisfaction. "Great," she said.

Emily said, "Where's a mirror? I want to see what you've done to me."

"No way, Emily. You've got to trust me. If you're worried about how you look, you won't be able to play. I need you to trust me." Her eyes bored into Emily's.

Somehow Emily realized that being trusted was very important to Caitlin. She said, "All right, friend. You got it. Let's get out there and play.

Wharton wasn't a good team. Their pitcher was lobbing the ball up there and the Ridge girls were pounding it, to the delight of the few parents and the dozen boys who were in attendance. Emily got up with two teammates on base and hit one over the fence to become an instant celebrity. Everybody laughed it up. It was fun, and when she checked on her eye makeup in the locker room after the game, she liked what she saw. The pale eye shadow made her blue eyes stand out and distracted attention from the tiny brown mole at the left corner of her mouth, which embarrassed her when she stopped to think about it. Her trust had been well placed.

The 16U basketball team had no fun and games, however. Everything was serious, even the team's name: the Morris Mauraders. Their first tournament was held at Kean College in Union. Teams from all over the state came to play. There were three games on Saturday, and possibly three more on Sunday, depending on their Saturday success. Now that the team was in their sleeveless game jerseys as opposed to the tee shirts they wore at practice, the tattoos on Mo's shoulder and the back of Ty's neck were visible. Mo's was a small spider-like creature drawn in a mixture of blue and green; Ty's was skull and crossbones. Both were repugnant to Emily.

Coach Booker was all about winning. She was also wise enough to know that a team could not win six games in two days playing only six or seven girls, so everybody got to play. Mo and Ty started in the front court along with Jo and Kelly at guard. Either One or Two started in the fifth spot. Emily couldn't tell them apart and wasn't sure the coach could either. Their main offense consisted of the fast break. Coach put in a stream of substitutes to keep fresh legs in the game and run the other team down. Emily got in two minutes before the end of the first quarter, replacing either One or Two; all she knew was that she replaced number fifteen.

The running game was fun for "Bones". She would get a rebound, pitch it out to a guard and sprint down the center of the court looking for a return pass. Those almost never came, and she would find herself fighting for the rebound of a teammate's shot. Sometimes she ended up on her butt, sometimes she got the ball and made some put backs but felt a little ignored. Still, They won their games on Saturday and two more on Sunday, which put them into the final.

The championship game in this tournament was against a huge team from New York City. The Mauraders got off to a slow start, which cut into the playing time of the subs. The game was rough. There were two referees who didn't seem too interested and let the big girls push and grab in the pivot as they wished. Tempers flared. Mo got into a wrestling match with her opponent, and both went down to the floor in a tangle of arms and legs amid a tirade of curses. Both players were ejected from the game. Coach Booker called time out.

Mo came to the bench head down and brushing at a small cut on her eyebrow. The coach ignored her. She put Emily into the game in place of Mo and changed up the offense. Emily would play at the foul line and from that high post position pass to the sides to Rene and Kelly, both in there to shoot threes. If there was no pressure on her she had permission to shoot, but priority when she turned to face the basket was to look for Ronna underneath. It was basically the same offense Ridge School had used to win the eighth-grade tournament.

Emily was delighted to get her hands on the ball more often. She felt comfortable in her role and worked hard to get herself open at the foul line when the guards had a chance to pass her the ball. The system worked well for a few minutes and the Mauraders closed the gap with a minute remaining. Their opponent adjusted their defense to take away the shots from the wing. Emily received a pass and turned to face the basket. Ronna was fronted by a giant girl under the basket, so Emily decided to shoot. The giant girl leaped at her, slapped the shot down court where one of their speedy guards grabbed it and scored a layup to ice the game. Emily was amazed. How could that girl have gotten from under the basket to block her shot so quickly? Her face got burning hot, and tears of embarrassment welled, which she wiped away with the back of a sweaty hand.

Coach Booker took her aside as the team collected their backpacks and coats.

"Welcome to the big time, Bones", she said. "Some of these kids are quicker and bigger than you've ever seen. Perhaps if you had faked the shot you could have passed the ball to Ronna when the shot-blocker jumped at you. Judging from your face, I think you'll remember that play without any need for video."

Emily stood there for a moment feeling her cheeks burn and was glad she had no eye makeup on today. She then joined the team huddle for a brief post game meeting. It was very brief. Coach looked at Mo and said, "See, Mo we got along just fine without you. Think about that. All right, practice Friday night at seven. We have some things to learn. Next Saturday's tournament is at Queens College Prep. We'll take the bus down and back."

The ride home was interminable. Her father lectured the whole way about how they could have won the last game. He particularly lambasted Mo for not being able to get beyond her "inner city" habits when it counted. Then he complained that the guards never threw Emily the ball and wondered if there was some kind of clique being formed. Emily just kept her mouth shut. She was looking forward to playing softball and having some fun tomorrow.

— — — — — — —

They were playing softball against Forsythe School. The game was a bit like a reprise of the basketball game they almost lost. Several girls on the softball team had played basketball. Indeed, the beefy girl who had harassed Emily for the whole basketball game was the Forsythe pitcher. And she was good. Each pitch seemed like a bullet to Emily, and she struck out three times.

After the third time the girl pointed at her and shouted, "Got you again." To get humiliated two days in a row was not fun for Emily. They lost 2-0.

Suzy patted her back. The boys razzed her a bit. She heard "the big swish" tossed her way. *At least she handled everything that came her way in the field* she thought, but that sounded lame to her. Most of the girls on the team smiled at the boys, but Emily could not.

━ ━ ━ ━ ━ ━

It took an hour to drive down to Queens College Prep on Saturday. The team traveled in a small bus borrowed from Morris Brown. Coach Booker drove. The format of the tournament was about the same except there would be only two games each day because there were fewer teams. Some of them were the same as the week before.

Mo did not start in the first game. She held her head up though and sat next to Emily on the bench. "Payin' my dues for loosin' my cool," she said. "I'm gonna have to play my way back in."

"Me too," said Emily. "I don't think I'll ever forget getting that shot blocked."

"You're kiddin'," replied Mo. "That kid already has a scholarship offer from North Carolina, and she's only a junior. You may never see anybody that good again."

"How do you know that?"

"Word gets around. It's like a big player's network on Facebook, Twitter and such."

"I feel left out."

"You're too young to worry yet."

Emily looked at Mo. "Sometimes I feel left out on the court too. I get open and somebody does a fancy spin-move to get off a shot but ignores me standing alone under the basket."

Mo took her eyes off the court for a moment and looked at Emily. "Bones, you gotta recognize that you're one of the new kids on the block and you're the baby of the bunch. The kids on the team who are gonna be juniors are lookin' to show their stuff. It's a critical year for gettin' the attention of college coaches. Your turn will come. Keep your head up."

Emily grunted. She felt like the baby of the bunch. A naive baby at that.

The Mauraders went on to win that tournament. Bones got to play a little more. In one game on Saturday, they went back to putting her at the high post to practice that system for whenever. She even got off two shots from the foul line that were not even close to being blocked. Maybe she was getting the feel of the game at this level.

While Emily was collecting her stuff after the last game and a brief team meeting, a short, dignified looking, gray-haired woman dressed in a charcoal gray business suit approached. She said, "I believe you are Emily Barker."

Startled, Emily just said, "Yes."

"And that you are still in eighth grade."

"Yes."

The woman smiled. "I'm Eva Laughlin. I'm the associate athletic director here. I assume your father is here somewhere. Fathers always come to see their daughters play. I'd like to talk to you both."

Emily had to smile. She said, "I thought my father was the only one so . . . obsessive. At least I don't have to ride that bouncy bus home. He's coming across the court now."

Ms. Laughlin greeted John with a warm handshake and invited them both to her office just off the gym. They sat across a beige steel desk from the AD. Pictures of the school's female basketball players and teams adorned every square foot of every wall.

The AD waved at the walls. "I coached the team here for many years. We were quite successful for a long time, but then some competitors began to recruit talent from afar. I got promoted to associate AD, and we joined the recruiting parade. We are improving our record, but still being out-gunned by some of our sister schools."

John said, "We saw the championship game a couple of weeks ago. Those teams were very talented. I believe they could have beaten most of the big public schools."

"Yes, I was there too. Very few of those players lived anywhere near either of those schools. We're changing our approach to recruiting students who happen to be skilled at sports. I'd like to offer Emily a full scholarship for four years at Queens College Prep."

"What!" said Emily.

John looked dumbfounded. "What brought this on?" he asked.

"Queens College Prep is a fine academic institution and has always been competitive athletically. Our graduates have traditionally gone to elite colleges and those have prepared them for careers that enriched society. We drew our students from families in the area that appreciated a superior education and the opportunities it offered. Many of their parents taught at nearby academic institutions or plied recognized professions. Now we are seeing a noticeable fraction of our students coming to the Prep from long distances and treating it as an apprenticeship for a professional athletic career. I'm trying to prevent our being labeled as one of those diploma mills you read about in *Sports Illustrated*."

"Even the Ivy League cultivates athletes," countered John.

"Yes, but those athletes can read and write, and they could when they got to ninth grade. We have to teach remedial courses in the three Rs well into tenth grade and the average test scores of our graduates has declined significantly. We're finding that many of our traditional potential students are turning up their noses at us because of our sagging academic reputation."

Emily started to squirm on her chair. Her father noticed.

"None of that explains why you are offering Emily a scholarship," said John.

"Sorry for being so long-winded," replied the AD. "In recent years I've launched a crusade to get the school back into the Ivy League model. I look for precocious athletes who are academically sound and offer them scholarships to attend our school. My attempt to rebuild our student body from the ground up has the support of our headmaster and the financial powers. Emily fits that model."

Emily and her father both stopped fidgeting and sat with their mouths open.

"What do you know about my academic record?" asked Emily.

"Queens College Prep grads are all over the state, as are my contacts in elementary schools. Those people tip me off to potential students and I follow up. We host many amateur sporting events here. Emily dribbled into my trap as it were."

Emily saw her father swell with pride as he had when Coach Booker had invited her to try out for the 16U team. He said, "Obviously this is a surprise, a shock even."

"Of course. As at other schools of this caliber, our total cost is over twenty thousand dollars per year. It would be entirely free for Emily."

It got so quiet in the room that Emily could hear her father breathe. The silence persisted for a full minute, to be interrupted by Ms. Laughlin. "Here's my card. I'd like to arrange for Emily to spend a full day here, attend some classes, meet some of her fellow athletes and the coach, and get all her questions answered. It's a big decision."

"Yes, it certainly is," answered John.

The woman stood and offered her hand first to John and then Emily. "Sleep on it for a few days, and then please call one way or the other."

"We'll do that," said John. "Thank you."

"Have a safe trip home."

Her father was totally quiet on the drive home. He said nothing about the game or the offer and seemed deep in thought. Emily was silent as well, her thoughts filled with pride, fear, and conflict. *She was going to have to make a decision about where to go to high school.*

Chapter Five

They arrived home just in time for dinner. John spent the entire meal filling Janet in on all the details of the scholarship offer, the highlights of which he had passed on in a cryptic illegal cell phone call as they drove home. Emily nibbled at the roast chicken and mashed potatoes and fidgeted in her seat seeking a way to escape and get to her phone and computer. At last, she remembered the old "homework" excuse and fled.

Two hours later Janet tapped on Emily's door. "What's the problem, lady? Your team won a championship and you got offered a scholarship. Seems like you should be celebrating, not nibbling at your dinner and fleeing to your room."

Emily sat on the end of her double bed, rumpling the gray bedspread with its yellow flowers that matched the color of the walls. She was slumped forward, her elbows on her knees. "Mom, winning the title was fine. The scholarship is scary."

"It's always nice to have options," said Janet, sitting on the bed next to Emily, grasping her shoulders and guiding her erect.

"The scholarship seems like a job. This Laughlin woman is on a crusade. I'd have to be a part of that. You know I've been up to my eyeballs in basketball since fifth grade. I see Suzy doing things that seem like fun that I don't have time for. I want to try some of those things."

"And you couldn't do that at Queens College Prep?"

"Not likely. It's an hour commute each way, and their web site implies that athletes have conditioning and such in the off season. It sounds like a training camp for college scholarships."

"A college scholarship would be nice. It costs fifty or sixty thousand a year almost everywhere these days."

"Depending on what happens in the next four years I may be ready to do that in college, but I don't think I want to do that in high school."

"What about the education opportunity?"

Emily had to smile at that. "Mom, you're the person who told me that I can get an excellent education anywhere if I apply myself. East Morris Regional sends kids to the Ivy League every year."

Janet laughed too. "I glad to hear that some of the things I say register. I assume you've shared your good fortune with Suzy and Caitlin and some others."

The smile ran away from Emily's face. "Yeah, and they were horrified."

"You realize, of course, that their first reaction is at least partly selfish. They don't want to lose your friendship."

"I never thought of it that way, but I don't want to lose them either."

"It's true that some of the closest friendships are formed in high school, but even those get diluted as our lives evolve. There are only three of my high school friends I keep in touch with now."

"Mom, I can't think that far ahead. I'm just hoping to get through the next six months in one piece."

"Yes, that's the priority. Turn your worries off and get some sleep. We'll talk some more soon." She bent over and kissed Emily on the forehead. "Ems, sometimes it's hard to be precocious at anything. All you can do is make the best choice possible at the time and evaluate it as time goes on."

"Oh, Mom."

"Yeah, I know. Sleep. The sun will come up tomorrow."

John got up early on workdays because he had to commute to Manhattan. Usually he was a slow starter, not able to find everything he needed, at least until Janet got a cup of coffee and half a bagel into him. Today, though, he had bounced out of bed, talking up a storm about the scholarship offer, projecting Ivy League scholarships in the future, and glorious headlines.

Janet remembered how he had been like this when he got appointed manager of his division over the head of a senior competitor. He had been filled with wonderful ideas for growing the business and future promotions. Some of that had worked out. Some hadn't, but his enthusiasm for his career dimmed only slightly. Now he was projecting it onto his daughter.

As John was slipping into his topcoat she said, "John, I don't want to throw a lot of cold water on the scholarship offer, but there are some drawbacks to an hour commute for a fourteen-year-old."

"Yeah, we'll need to work out the transportation issue. I have some ideas."

"Just don't get carried away making plans. There's a lot to think about before any decision."

John looked at her the way he did when she suggested a camping vacation. "Gotta go," he said, kissed her gently, and rushed out the door into the garage.

Emily came into the kitchen with her softball gear in a duffle bag about a half hour later. "Morning, Mom."

"Good morning, Ems. Did you sleep OK?"

"It took a while, but once I got to sleep, I was out of it. Almost didn't hear the alarm."

"You have a softball game today I see. Is it at home?"

"Yeah. Can you come?"

"I plan to. I also made some pancakes for us."

Emily looked at the clock on the microwave. "I have to be quick."

Janet put a stack of three pancakes, drowned in real maple syrup and a glass of milk in front of her daughter. "You have to keep up your strength. You didn't have much dinner last night, and it's going to be another long day."

"Thanks, Mom. I hope I can at least get my bat on the ball today."

"If you concentrate you can do anything."

Between mouthfuls Emily said, "With all the stuff that's going on in my head concentrating will be hard."

"Try to block out all that stuff for a day or so. Trying to hit the ball might help. The girls on the team will be cheering for you too."

"And the boys will be razzing me if I fail."

"Even that should take your mind off what you think of as a problem. Some people would call it an opportunity."

Emily stopped with a forkful of pancakes halfway to her mouth. "Are you going to push the scholarship on me too?"

"No, Ems. I'm just trying to help you get that particular choice in perspective. It's early days. No need to rush into anything."

"The lady asked us to call back in a couple of days."

"We can always say we're still thinking about it."

"I guess," said Emily. "I gotta go or I'll miss the bus. See you at the game."

"I'll be there." Janet didn't really want to sit at any game on what promised to be a chilly afternoon, but considering Emily's unease, she knew she'd have to be there. Maybe watching the game would help her put her own thoughts in perspective.

Despite being dressed in short sleeves and short pants Emily felt warm surrounded by her teammates in their makeup. She needed to get some of her own, not piggyback on Caitlin. They were excited about the game. They always liked to beat Mendham. The energy of that rubbed off on Emily. She felt a part of something, just as she did on the basketball court.

Mendham had a good pitcher. She didn't throw as hard as the beefy girl from Forsythe but mixed in a nasty change up to keep batters off balance. She was more than too much for Emily, who struck out her first two times up. Suzy and Caitlin at least got the bat on the ball when they got up, but got no hits, and neither team scored a run.

The game raced along getting to the last half of the sixth inning in only an hour. It was almost Ridge's last chance to win in regulation. Emily was scheduled to bat first in the inning. Suzy put her arm around Emily as the pitcher took her warmup throws.

"Why don't you try to bunt?" she suggested.

Emily was so frustrated about trying to hit the ball she never thought about bunting. "I'm not sure that I can even do that," she said.

"She throws at least one change up to every batter. Forget the fastballs, wait for the change, stick your bat in front of it, and run like the devil was after you."

Emily felt that she had nothing to lose. She went up there trying to look as menacing as possible but kept the bat on her shoulder until the count got to be one ball and two strikes. There had been no change ups so far. She had to do something on the next pitch.

The Mendham pitcher knew that too. She came with the slow one, guessing that Emily would be on a quick trigger.

Wrong! Emily stuck the bat out and made contact. The ball rolled about halfway to the pitcher and ten feet to her right. Emily sprinted for first with the same determination she used in leading a fast break to the basket. Janet had been huddled on the frigid aluminum bleachers; her arms wrapped around her middle against the cold. Now she jumped off her seat and screamed, "Run, Ems. Go!"

Unfortunately, Emily was a half-step too slow. She was out, but somehow felt exhilarated by the effort. Maybe if she had gotten the ball to roll a couple of feet more toward third base, she would have made it. Suzy gave her a big hug when she got back to the dugout

The other Ridge batters went down in order. And the game slipped away in the next inning, when Caitlin bobbled a grounder, Mendham bunted the runner to second successfully, and their catcher got a clean base hit to score the run. Revitalized, their pitcher mowed down the home team in the bottom half of the inning to lock up the win.

Everybody hugged Caitlin in the dugout after the game. She was weepy but perked up when the boys came by to say things like "Great game." "Way to give those big heads all they could handle." "We'll get them next time." Emily felt the support, the camaraderie of the group even in the loss. That stuff didn't exist for her on the AAU circuit.

Emily checked out her eye makeup in the mirror in the passenger side sunshade when she made it to the car. It looked fine. She did indeed like how it highlighted her eyes.

Her mother said, "You were almost safe on the bunt. It was a great effort."

"Almost doesn't count, but it did feel good to hit the ball."

Janet contemplated her daughter for a moment then asked, "Where did you get the eye shadow?"

"Caitlin. There's a tradition for the eighth graders to wear it. I need to get something of my own, but I have no idea how to put it on, so I'll still have to rely on Caitlin."

Janet laughed and said, "I'm sure I can help you with that. I gather the boys in the stands like to see their team look pretty."

"The boys are not really important to me, Mom, but I do want to be part of the team."

"The boy part will change sometime, Ems. Enjoy the camaraderie for now." Janet felt a little warm feeling in her stomach. She thought, *getting her uniform clean after a game is a pain, but Emily's being on the softball team may be opening her eyes a bit.*

John had to entertain a client that night, so there was no discussion of the "thing" to ruin dinner. Emily felt that some of the weight of the world had been lifted from her shoulders. She and her mother ran out to CVS to get some eye shadow. Janet taught her how to apply it tastefully. She did her homework, exchanged some text messages with Suzy and Caitlin, found out that they both liked classmate Billy Pedrazi and saw problems ahead, but went right to sleep.

The next evening Emily's father got home a little early and dinner was going to be a little late, so he suggested they go out in the backyard and use the extra hour of daylight provided by daylight-saving time to work on some of the new footwork she had been taught at AAU practice.

At this Emily said, "I've got a better idea, Dad. Let's go up to the batting cages on Route 10."

"Why is that a better idea?" asked her father.

"Cause I'm tired of striking out."

That shut her father up for a minute. Emily was sure that he wanted to say that batting was not important for her future but felt good that he knew enough not to. That eased some of the tension between them.

He said, "OK, let's see if I can help with that."

Emily went upstairs to get her batting gloves and the bat her family had paid $200 for and was still unmarked. They got to the batting cages and found that the pitching machines offered three speeds. At ten pitches for a dollar. John pulled out his wallet. "I don't have any singles to stick in the machine. I'll go get some change."

"I brought some," said Emily. "Let's try the medium speed machine."

Her father said, "Wow. You brought your own money? This is important."

Emily had to smile. She said, "I thought playing on the softball team would just be a social thing, fun and games. It turns out I can't put up with my being, you know, a klutz. I have to do the best I can no matter what."

"All right, my little tiger. Did you know that I played on my high school baseball team? Maybe I know something that can help."

So, Emily got into the right-hand batter's box in the medium speed cage and her father stepped into the empty one next to it so he could get a side view of her attempts to hit the ball. Not every pitch was near enough to the strike zone to be hittable, but Emily swung at all of them because her problem was getting the bat to contact the ball.

After the first ten pitches were exhausted, her father suggested that she take a much shorter stride at the start of her swing. "They always told me not to lunge at the ball and to trust my hands," he said. "Concentrate on trying to see the bat hit the ball."

That helped a little. Emily got the bat on five of the next ten pitches, but her father's face was lined with concentration. He said, "Some people have one eye that's dominant over the other. Do you think you would have beaten out the bunt the other day if you were a left-hand batter?"

"I was out by less than a full step. It could be."

"This time try batting left-handed."

"I've never done that."

"Humor your old man, please."

Emily went back into the cage on the other side of the plate.

"Just bunt the first few pitches," her father instructed.

She did that and managed to get her bat in front of four of the first five pitches.

"Not bad," her father. "Now take a short swing. Don't move your feet. Just flick the bat at the ball with your wrists. Trust your hands."

Again, she hit four of the five pitches, two of them solidly. She felt clumsy; couldn't swing the bat very hard but had to admit the results were better. "Let's try some more from here," she said, her face a mask of concentration.

And so they did. She got a little more comfortable with each swing. Her bat met the ball more solidly more of the time. She thought her father had put her on to something.

"I don't know what our coach will say if I get up left-handed on Friday, but I'm going to try it. Thanks, Dad.

"Anything to help my little darling be her best."

When they were in the car for the trip home John asked, "Can we talk about the scholarship for a minute?"

"No"

"No? I have to call the AD tomorrow."

"I really can't see commuting an hour each way to go to high school, Dad."

"Suppose we just set a date for a visit. No commitments. I'll take a day off from work and we'll all go."

Emily saw her father working the scholarship problem step by step, just as he had her batting problem. It had felt good to work with her father on her hitting. Maybe they could work the same way on this other, really big, thing.

"OK, Dad we'll visit, but I don't want to miss any softball games."

- - - - - -

It was early May, but a late April shower washed out practice on the field on Thursday. The team went into the gym, threw a little, and practiced dealing with rundowns. The topic of Emily batting left-handed never came up.

Friday's game went on as scheduled. The Randolph Middle School had a turf field. Emily was the tallest girl on the Ridge team but was batting last in the lineup in contrast to where big girls batted on most teams. At least the coach didn't put in a designated player to hit for her. She walked to the plate for her first at bat in the top of the third inning with her team losing one to nothing and stepped into the left-hand batter's box. She had said absolutely nothing about trying to hit left-handed, not even a word to Suzy and Caitlin. Her coach, Jack Connel, took one look, yelled for time out, and ran toward home plate.

"Emily, what do you think you're doing?"

"Well, coach, I can't seem to even hit the ball batting righty, you know, so my father and I went to the cages Wednesday, and I seemed to do better batting lefty."

"I'd much rather you try this out in practice first."

"It rained yesterday and I'm tired of striking out."

Her coach was quiet long enough for the umpire to chuckle and say, "That's why they pay you so much, coach. Can we get on with the game, please?"

"I hate to say this, Emily, but you're right about one thing. There's not much to lose. Give it your best shot."

He jogged back to the third base coaching box and shouted, "Go get them, Big E."

Suzy and Caitlin picked up the cry and soon the entire team was up in the dugout chanting "Go Big E."

Emily had to smile at that, but the first pitch wiped the smile off her face. This skinny, red-haired girl threw faster than anyone she had seen before and faster than the medium speed machine at the cages. Still, she thought she saw the ball better than in previous games. Her pulse ramped up. She dug her left foot into the carpet of the batter's box and focused.

Emily slapped at the next pitch and fouled it back. Suzy yelled, "You're right on it, E. Get the next one!"

Emily fouled off the next pitch too. And the next; and the one after that. She felt pretty good about getting her bat on a pitch three times in a row. On top of that she thought that the pitcher was looking frustrated, as if she was not used to having so much trouble getting the last batter in any lineup out.

Emily asked for time and stepped out of the box, figuring the delay would add to the pitcher's irritation. Perhaps she was right. The next pitch was high, ball one. Then one came right down the middle. Emily made contact, the ball rolling slowly toward shortstop. The third baseman ran to cut it off but stopped when the shortstop yelled for it.

Emily ran as if her pants were on fire. She beat the throw to first and leaped into the air at the umpire's call of "Safe". It was the first time she had gotten on base in the last seven games. The rest of the team chanted, "Way to go, Big E." Caitlin and Suzy pounded each other on the back. Their coach just shook his head with a big grin on his face.

The Randolph pitcher was thoroughly annoyed. She walked the Ridge leadoff hitter, the smallest girl on the team, and her coach came out to calm her down. The next batter struck out, but Caitlin hit a ground ball back past the pitcher which bounced into center field. Emily raced toward third base, where her coach gave her the stop sign. Emily shifted into overdrive. This might be the only chance she would ever have to score a run and she was not about to pass it up. She flew around third base and sprinted for home.

She and the throw from the center fielder arrived at about the same time. Emily slid hard, her left foot slamming into the shin guard on the thick left leg of the catcher. The force of it knocked the leg out from under the catcher and she fell on top of Emily in a cloud of the small bits of rubber that were the base of the turf field.

A split-second later Emily heard the home-plate umpire roar "Safe". She screamed "Yeah!" The umpire helped the disgruntled catcher up off Emily, and she leaped to her feet, to be pounded and hugged by her teammates as enthusiastically as if she had scored the winning run in the league championship.

Once the excitement spent itself, things went back to near normal. Randolph scored two more runs in the sixth inning to go ahead 3-1. Emily got up again in the top of the seventh and hit the ball again. This time it went right back to the pitcher, who threw her out at first with plenty of time to spare.

The bus ride back home was a mixed bag. Coach Connel was not happy about losing another close game but had some hopes for the remaining games on their schedule. Maybe they could make the playoffs. The girls, some of them anyway, were in a party mood. One grabbed Emily's visor and passed it up and down the aisle, evading her laughing attempts to reclaim it. She also got abused because the slide into home messed up her eye shadow.

Suzy shouted, "Too bad we were playing on the road. The guys would have loved to see that slide. That was the Big E we know."

Emily just laughed. If her father had been there, he would have had a heart attack looking at the slide. A trip to the emergency room and missing the last month of the AAU basketball season would have been all he saw. No such fears ever entered Emily's mind. All this celebration and horsing around was fun, but deep inside her she realized that she knew only one way to play anything: full bore.

At dinner that night her father asked about the afternoon's game.

Emily answered with a big smile. "We lost 3-1, but I batted lefty. I hit the ball both times I got up, got a hit, and scored the only run we got. It was awesome."

Her father laughed. "What did your coach say about batting lefty?"

"He almost wet his pants. Finally, he agreed that there wasn't much to lose and said I should go for it. I think your dominant eye theory was right."

John's face got serious. "Glad of that. Let me tell you what else I've done that I hope is right. I made a date for all of us to visit Queens College Prep on June 17. I checked. That's just after your graduation, but they still have school."

Emily looked at her mother with her mouth open. All she said was "OK," but her face spoke volumes. Janet could almost feel the stress rising in her daughter's chest but said nothing.

The next three weeks went by in tornado of activity. The weather got warmer. The softball team continued its 0.500 season. She was hitting the ball fairly regularly from the left side and had been moved up higher in the batting order, but the team did not make the playoffs. She was not happy about that because she was beginning to enjoy softball and the cheers of the boys.

On the AAU basketball circuit Emily was seeing more playing time and more acceptance from her teammates. On negative side, the gyms in which they played were becoming increasingly overheated from the sun shining through high windows. It was not unusual for players to require a lot of hydration to avoid leg cramps or light-headedness during the second or third game of the day. Emily lost a couple of much needed pounds each weekend and came home exhausted.

Chapter Six

Graduation from Ridge Middle School was traditionally held on its expansive front lawn. This year students, teachers, parents, and relatives were blessed with a beautiful evening. The timing of the event was early enough so that it could be completed before dark, when the mosquitoes came out. Spectators sat on white folding chairs nicely lined up on the lush grass and focused on the stage. A set of bleachers was set to the left to accommodate the school chorus and the school band occupied an area to the right of the stage.

The Barkers had gotten there early enough to find seats in the center of the second row for Janet, John, and Janet's parents from Manhattan, for whom it was the first grandchild graduation they had ever attended. Janet was their only child. It would have been the first for John's parents as well, but they were older and had retired to Florida some years ago.

The graduates marched in aligned in size places; the boys in green gowns, most showing neckties; the girls wore buttoned up white gowns. They walked quickly down the central aisle, perhaps anxious to consummate their rite of passage. The boys walked in one line partnered by a mostly taller girl. The school band played the traditional "Pomp and Circumstance". There were ninety-one kids in the class, a dozen of color. The adults applauded politely, but those with younger siblings were often greeted with raucous cheers.

Emily was the tallest girl, even though she wore her Sunday church shoes with a half inch heel and many others wore two-inch-high platform shoes. Since there were three more girls than boys in the class, she was the last graduate in the line, just behind a pair of girls. One of those girls was only an inch shorter than she, African American, and in no way athletic.

She was going to receive an award for excellence in literature. The contrast between that girl and the black players on her AAU team suddenly struck Emily. She also realized that she knew little about most of her class, and not even the names of some of them. Her devotion to basketball and athletics in general caused a space between them which seemed strange in this last act of community. She felt alone, a geek at the end of the line, and was glad that they were moving fast so that she could soon lose herself in the mass of white gowns on the bleachers behind the podium.

Emily was an excellent student, but not the best in any individual class. Thus, she got none of the individual awards for academic excellence. She was among the one-third of the class that got a certificate from the federal government for achieving a grade point average of at least 3.75 out of 4. She and Billy Pedrazi each got awards for sportsmanship and athletic achievement though. Clutching her plaque, which had been donated by a major sporting goods store, she thought, *here I am branded as a jock. Where is that going to leave me?*

She forgot her worries about the future in the embrace of her mother, the back pounding of her father and gentile hugs of her grandparents. The whole group went to a small restaurant in Madison for a celebratory dinner.

One of the beauties of New Jersey is that many restaurants are BYOB: bring your own bottle. John brought more than enough for the adults. Soon the conversation was well lubricated.

Janet's father turned to Emily and said," Congratulations on your basketball award. I understand that you have been offered a scholarship to play at a fine prep school."

"Well, yes, but the school is pretty far away."

"Your mother had to travel a pretty good distance to her prep school in Manhattan when she was your age," he replied.

Janet interrupted. "That was true, but I traveled with friends on the subway. I would have to drive Ems there."

Janet's father turned to her and raised his eyebrows. "Isn't any effort worth your child's getting the best education possible? Those schools have connections to the best colleges. Look at your experience at Barnard."

Janet laughed. "That included having to go to basketball games at Manhattan for some excitement."

"Several kids from our local high school go to the Ivy League every year," said Emily.

Perhaps a little defensively John said, "You can get a great education at any school if you put your mind to it."

"John, you know it's not the same," said his father-in-law. "You've had to climb over some Ivy Leaguers to get to where you are. It would have been easier if you had the elite stamp on your forehead."

"I rest my case," said John.

"Don't you want things to be easier for Emily?"

Janet jumped in to change the subject. She had seen such debates between her husband and her father escalate into serious arguments. She said, "Ems are you friends with Billy Pedrazi?"

Emily was quick to respond. "Sort of. We're basketball buddies. I think both Caitlin and Suzy are more interested in him socially. He's pretty tall for Caitlin and Suzy is not much into sports, but I don't want get in the way of their interest."

Her grandmother asked, "Isn't it pretty early in life to be worried about that kind of stuff?"

"For me it is, but I'm a little different. Still, the kids I hang out with are all my friends, Grandma. It's fun to be with them and chill. I don't want that to change."

"Everything is bound to change sooner or later," said Grandpa.

"All the more reason to enjoy things while you can," said Janet. "Ah, here come our dinners."

The food was excellent. Conversation ranged from how things were going in New Jersey, to the potential traffic problems caused by Uber drivers in Manhattan, to the weather forecast for the summer, and the classes Emily would take in high school. Everybody left full and happy, and early enough to drive home without stress.

At home Janet went to say good night to Emily. Her daughter was looking grim as she fiddled with her smart phone on her bed.

"You don't look like a happy graduate, I'm sad to say."

"Mom, Grandpa just upped the pressure on the scholarship at dinner tonight. Do you believe that getting a prep school education is the key to success?"

"No. I got one and went to an elite college. At least it was one then. Your father didn't. Are we hurting for anything?"

"Not that I know of. Are there other things I don't know about?"

"Other things?"

"Well, I know you color your hair. Is there something else?"

Janet laughed. "Caught in the act. Parents always have a few secrets from their 14-year-old daughters, and don't forget we're learning about this job as we go. Things will work out, Hon. You're off to a good start in life, and we'll do our best to prevent anything from knocking you off that path."

"Thanks, Mom.

"Sleep well. Summer is here."

"Not quite, Mom. Still some work to do."

Janet kissed Emily on the forehead, sighed, and went to bed thinking *so serious, so young. I need to help her loosen up if I can.*

— — — — — — —

It rained the day they visited Queens College Prep, so Ms. Laughlin arranged an oversize golf cart to transport them to each of the several buildings that made up the campus. Aside from the athletic complex, many buildings were Gothic, wood paneled and quite elegant inside. The classrooms and laboratories were modern and the class sizes they observed were small. The Barkers got to sit in on parts of two classes. Emily had to admit that those teachers were a cut above what she had in Ridge Middle School.

Lunch was part of the normal service supplied by the school. They ate in the cafeteria amid a crowd of boisterous and seemingly happy students. Ms. Laughlin introduced Emily to several female athletes who seemed quite nice. Then they went to meet the girls' basketball coach and a few of the team at the gym.

The coach was named Sean Burnside, a large black man who had played his college ball at Wake Forest. He was six feet-six inches tall and must have weighed close to 250 pounds. Emily thought *I'd hate having him mad at me.*

Sean was dressed in a red polo shirt which bore the Queens College Prep logo and looked like it was silk. This was matched with sharply pressed khaki trousers and white Under Amour basketball shoes trimmed with red. He looked as if he were ready for a TV sound bite.

Sean spoke for some time about his approach to coaching and how it served not only to bring success to the school program, but also how it prepared his players for college careers. Emily asked, "How many of your graduates go on to play in college?"

He answered, "About half of those who play regularly on our varsity team go on to play in college. We have three teams: freshman, JV, and varsity. There are 12 full time members on the varsity squad, mostly juniors and seniors. Sometimes we bring up one or two of the JV's to get some experience against some of our weaker opposition. Generally, half of the varsity players are on scholarship, as are several of the freshman and JV players."

John asked, "All in, how many scholarship basketball players are there in any one year?"

"Normally twelve. Ms. Laughlin is trying to increase that number a little, hoping to add what she calls 'some balance' to the program. However, even with just 12 scholarship players it's a little difficult to keep all of them happy at the level of success we're striving for."

"Do you recruit all of the scholarship players personally?" asked Emily.

"No. Ms. Laughlin coached here for a long time and uses that experience to recommend some of them."

John stiffened. "How do you feel about those players?"

Sean smiled. "They are generally an asset to the program. They're smart, work at least as hard as our best players, and even those who don't grow into the starting lineup, are very valuable contributors to our preparations for the big games."

There was a moment of silence during which Emily tried to catch her father's eye unsuccessfully.

Sean broke the silence. "Several of our varsity players are in the gym involved in our off- season conditioning program. Would you like to meet them?"

Emily said, "Absolutely."

There was a ball laying on the gym floor as they left Sean's office Emily picked it up took one dribble and lofted a shot from the foul line. Nothing but net.

"Showing off?" asked Sean.

"Since you may never have seen me play, it couldn't hurt."

Sean smiled. "The weight room is this way," he said.

A half-dozen students was in the weight room. Two of the basketball players were immediately obvious. Two black girls taller than six feet were spotting each other with what looked like more than 100 pounds on the bar. They were being egged on by another clearly athletic girl who was a couple of inches shorter than Emily but was more muscular.

Sean called out to the trio, "Girls, come say hello to Emily Barker. She may be joining our program next year."

The girl with the bar bounced it down on the wooden platform at the weight station with a monumental thud, and they all came over. Names were exchanged, and everybody smiled. Sean said, "I'll leave you all to chat a bit. Bring Emily to my office when you're done, please."

"Sure, coach," replied one of the big girls.

"Where are you from, Emily," asked the smaller player.

"Florham Park."

"Where the hell is that?" asked the girl who was lifting the weight when they arrived.

Janet answered, "A few miles east of Morristown."

"I've heard of Morristown," said the second big girl. "Something about Washington hanging out there during the Revolution, but I've never been there. I'm from Newark."

The smaller girl gestured toward the weightlifter. "Amanda and I are from Trenton. All three of us will be seniors next year. Amanda already has a scholarship offer from Pittsburgh. We're all playing AAU this summer in hopes of more offers. Emily, didn't I see you playing here a few weeks ago?"

"Yeah, I'm playing on the Mauraders, a 16U team. We're going off to a big tournament in Pittsburgh this summer. All that is new to me. I'm the baby on the team."

"That's tough. Those big tournaments are mostly time to show off for college coaches. It's tough for younger players to even get the ball. Did Coach Sean invite you here?"

"No. Ms. Laughlin did."

"Oh."

"Oh, what?' asked John.

The girls looked at each other. The shorter one shrugged. "There's a little friction between those two. A couple of the girls she's brought in haven't measured up."

Janet entered the conversation. "Haven't measured up, or haven't been given a chance to measure up?"

The girl looked at Janet. "A couple of them were too nice. They got pushed around and quit, but there was one girl who gave me fits in practice, but only got to play in garbage time. She hung in there and she's going to play at Gettysburg next year."

"That was true of a big white girl from somewhere in northwest Jersey," added the girl from Newark. "We'd bang heads every day, but she only got to play when I got in foul trouble, which I learned not to do pretty fast."

"Is he scary to play for?" asked Emily.

"Let's just say it's not good around here if we lose."

The shorter girl spoke to Emily. "Look, I watched you play for a bit in that game a few weeks ago. You're pretty good. Unless you grow some more, you won't be playing in the paint here, and wherever you play you need to beef up a little, but you probably know that already. There's some competition for you already here. If you want a real challenge, come here ready to fight."

A light went off in Emily's head. "Where are you going to college?"

"Princeton. Yeah, I'm one of Coach Burnside's recruits that Ms. Laughlin approves of."

Janet said, "Girls, thank you very much for talking with us so honestly. We obviously have some heavy thinking to do."

The girls said, "No problem. Good luck," almost in unison.

CHAPTER SEVEN

Emily sat in the back of their car for the trip home as she always did. Janet started the discussion while John concentrated on negotiating the somewhat circuitous path out of the parking lot onto Easton Avenue. "We're not going to talk about this visit tonight, and Emily has at least two games tomorrow at East Stroudsburg. That's a long ride, and there's nothing on the schedule for Sunday. So . . . we're going to church on Sunday morning like normal people, maybe Ems can get her place back in the choir, and then we'll go to the diner for brunch. That's when we'll talk about Queens College Prep and high school."

"What's the matter with talking about it tonight while it's fresh?" asked John.

"Because it's too fresh. We need time to digest what we learned and maybe pray over a decision. Because of all the games we haven't been to church in a while."

John bit his lip. Emily was deeply relieved. She wanted time to think and talk with her friends.

About half-way home Emily's phone dinged. It was a text message from Caitlin. It read, "You're not going there, are you?"

Emily typed back, "Family conference Sun."

She wasn't looking forward to that.

—————

The trip to East Stroudsburg took an hour and a half. A caravan of five cars, four of them driven by doting parents, left the Morris Brown School at seven AM. Mo rode with Emily's folks. Coach Booker drove those who didn't hook up with one of the other cars.

They played three games in a blistering hot field house holding four courts side-by-side, laid out across the main, full-sized court. The Mauraders won the first two easily, which delighted Emily because she got to play a lot. The third game was harder, but they won, and Emily played three quarters of the game as their coach saved the starters for the finals.

The tournament committee reconfigured the court so that the final game was played on the full-size college court. It was twenty feet longer than the courts on which the preliminary games had been played. In the heat, that change took its toll on all the players. The Marauders jumped ahead early but seemed to run out of gas. Their opponent was the host team, which may have had some experience playing on the big court.

Coach Booker tried various combinations, including Emily and some other subs, but no combination could put the game away. They struggled to the finish, winning by eight as a result of a bevy of fouls shots near the end.

The normally perfunctory post game talk was anything but. Coach raved on about over confidence, lack of killer instinct, lack of conditioning, and how, if they played that way at the big tournament in Pittsburgh next weekend, they wouldn't make it past the first cut. She finished with, "To fix that we're going to have practice tomorrow morning as well as Thursday night. Go home and think about your performance today. Get determined to play better next weekend."

Emily wondered what to do. She was looking forward to playing in Pittsburgh but needed to get the Queens College Prep thing behind her. Breaking up her mother's plan to get that done because of the dominance of a basketball practice would break her heart. On the other hand, telling Coach Booker that she was not going to make practice tomorrow right now, even though she had never missed one, was not a good idea either. Coach was thoroughly pissed. Maybe she just wouldn't show up and claim to have been sick or dehydrated or something.

She dawdled at collecting her backpack and warm-ups. Mo grabbed her arm. "What's up?" she asked.

Emily told her.

"Get your old man to tell her."

"He might not do that."

"You want me to go with you?"

That stopped Emily short. Here was this black girl from Newark, who had no connection with her other than the team, who was two years older with an infinite amount of street smarts, offering to take the risk with her of facing an angry coach with bad news.

Emily said, "Mo, thanks a lot. That's great of you to offer, but I think I gotta do this myself, you know. Catch up with my folks. I'll be with you in a minute."

She caught up with Coach Booker as she was leaving the gym with the three members of the team she had driven to the tournament. "Coach, can I talk to you a minute?"

"Sure, Emily but make it quick. It's a long drive home."

"You know I've never missed a practice, right?"

"So?"

Emily took a deep breath and just blurted it out. "I can't come to practice tomorrow."

"Why the hell not?"

"My mother has planned a special family thing for tomorrow, since the original schedule was open."

"And that's more important than preparing for our biggest tournament of the year? Maybe the tournament is not important to you either."

Emily's eyes got wide. "It is, coach. It is. I just gotta do this thing. It's really important."

"Bones, what's so important that you're willing to risk the trip to Pittsburgh?"

Emily looked at her feet, then locked eyes with her coach. "We have to decide whether I'm going to accept a scholarship to Queens College Prep."

"Ha," said Coach Booker. "I saw the AD corner you and your father that day we played down there. So that's what that was all about."

"Yeah. We went down there to visit Friday. They want an answer by Monday."

"Do you know that there is some in-fighting going on in that program?"

"Yeah. We had a good talk with several of the girls on the team."

"Do you still want to go?"

"Not really, but one of the girls we talked to is going to Princeton. If I got to go there it would make my parents really happy."

"What do you know about Princeton?"

"Nothing really."

"Princeton is a big name, a huge name. There's no doubt that a degree from there can open some doors for you. When I was in college, I played against Princeton. Those girls didn't seem any happier or smarter than any other team I played against. Before you get all excited about the distant future, you had better face up to what's good for you right now."

She studied Emily's face for a long moment. "OK you're off the hook for tomorrow. Find some time to practice your foul shots before Thursday. You missed two today."

Emily let out a deep breath. "Thanks, Coach. I will."

Mo intercepted her halfway to her parents. "How did it go?"

Emily was still breathing a bit heavily, but she smiled. "She started off mad, but then listened. I think she may not be as mean as she acts. I'm good for tomorrow. We don't need to say anything about this on the ride home though, right?

Mo smiled. "You'll owe me for that."

"OK."

Chapter Eight

The Barker family waited a few minutes so that they could sit at a corner booth in the crowd at the Florham Park diner on Sunday shortly before noon. The room was redolent of frying butter and fat. Luxurious deserts filled a case next to where they waited.

Once settled in the maroon vinyl covered cushions, they spent a quiet minute studying the five-page menu. John ordered a cheeseburger, but Janet and Emily went for the pancakes. That done, Janet asked, "Ems, do you want to go to Queens College Prep?"

"No."

"And why not," asked her father.

"There are a lot of reasons. First, I don't want to commute for an hour to get to high school and put Mom through all that trouble. Second, I don't want to be the flag bearer for the AD in her war against the coach. Third, I want to go to high school with my friends. Is that enough?"

"I see that you've been thinking a lot about this. What about the chance to get a great education and go to Princeton, Yale, or some other elite school?" pressed her father.

"If I work at it, I can get a great education anywhere. Kids from East Morris Regional go to the Ivy League.

"Most of those are Asian," retorted her father.

"So what? Don't you think I have the brains to compete?"

"Of course, you do," answered her father after looking away for a moment. "It's just that with all the time you put in at basketball it will be hard to do all the work needed to get A's."

"What about all the time I would have to spend commuting and the time I would have to spend in the gym off-season?"

John was quiet for a moment, so Janet jumped in. "I checked. EMR offers almost all the AP courses Queens College Prep does accept for Advanced Calculus and fourth year French. There should be plenty of opportunity to pad her academic resume."

Emily heaved a major sigh. "Come on Mom. Let me get past Algebra II and Language Arts before you force Calculus on me. I want to take Choir too."

John said, "We need to think about the basketball program too. EMR hasn't won the county championship in ten years; hasn't even made it to the semi-finals since they had that big Breslin girl six years ago."

"I heard she went on to play at Georgetown," countered Emily.

"One in a thousand," said her father. "For that to happen, your coach must have connections. The current girls' basketball coach is a baseball guy. He coaches the JV baseball team. His father coaches the varsity team. He doesn't have time to watch any AAU games. He probably knows nothing about you even now."

Emily shrugged. "So what? Coach Costello will give him a heads up, and I'll just have to get his attention on the court. After all I've worked at this summer, that shouldn't be too hard."

The food arrived and they all dug in for a few minutes.

Janet asked between mouthfuls, "Ems, how much of your thinking is based on social aspects as opposed to the opportunity?"

"I don't know, Mom. I love basketball. I want to be the best I can be, skinny nerd that I am. But basketball can't be my whole life; can't control everything I do, and going to high school with my friends would feel good."

Janet sat up straight with a big smile. Clearly Emily had pushed one of her main parental buttons. "Emily, you've had your period for over a year now. You're not likely to grow much taller. If you look at your parents, it should be clear that you won't be skinny much longer. You'll start to blossom and have to struggle to stay quick enough to play your best, but from what I've seen this summer, a little beef in your butt might help you."

John raised his hands in surrender. This was beyond anything he could deal with. He said, "I think your reservations about getting into the middle of any feud at Queens are very real. If you go to EMR, we're going to have work the AAU circuit hard to make up for the coach's lack of connections."

Emily's eyes started to fill. She reached across the table to grasp her father's hand. "Dad, I appreciate your going along with me on this. I promise I'll work hard at basketball and do my best in class. I'm gonna spread my wings a little in high school though."

John looked down at his half-empty plate and muttered, "I guess we all did."

CHAPTER NINE

Emily shot 200 foul shots before Thursday night's practice came. She felt pretty good about that when she got to the gym, but Coach Booker never asked about that. Nor did she ask about the Queens College Prep decision. She was totally focused on preparations for the upcoming tournament.

To that end, she had brought in five boys from the Morris Brown team to play defense while her squad practiced breaking various kinds of press defenses. They stayed on while some new throw-in plays were learned. Emily got knocked down a couple of times when she set a screen on a good-looking boy who had to be forty pounds heavier than she. He apologized, smiled, and helped her up both times. That relieved some of the pain in her ribs and butt. She realized that her mother was right about some well-placed additions to her physique

Their coach then sat them down on the bleachers for some instructions. "We're going to be playing college rules in Pittsburgh. We'll have a 30 second shot clock and the semi-circle under the basket for secondary defenders looking to take a charge. More than that, there will be three officials on every game. They'll all have college officiating experience and will be trying out for spots on the ACC and Northeast conference staffs. They won't be those lazy clowns we've been seeing at some of the local tournaments. They'll be refereeing the hell out of every game, so I've brought in a couple of friends of mine to referee a scrimmage here tonight. Hopefully we'll purge ourselves from sloppy screens, hand checks, push offs and the like.

"I expect this will give us an edge. There are 32 teams in this tournament, split into four groups. Losers of their first game get dumped into a consolation bracket. They get to play another game, but who wants to play for fifth place in some group? If we win the first two games, we get to play in the group final Saturday evening. Group champions play in the tournament semifinal Sunday morning, and the winner of that plays in the final in the afternoon. Everybody else just sits and watches. I don't like watching. Let's get to work."

There were only two refs for the scrimmage, but they blew up a storm. After about a half hour of seemingly endless whistles, the team started to get the message. By the end of an hour the frequency of foul calls had decreased to a tolerable level. It was a level of training Emily had never thought any coach would undertake. As the scrimmage went on both Coach and the referees gave some demonstrations of how to achieve the same result that a foul might provide without getting charged with an illegal act.

After practice Coach Booker had a last instruction. "We're leaving here at nine tomorrow morning in a small bus borrowed from the school. As instructed at Sunday's practice, I trust you have all cleared being absent from school tomorrow with the appropriate school officials. We should get to the Ramada Inn in time for dinner and our first game is at nine on Saturday at U. Pitt. Any questions?"

There were none.

"What about you, Bones? Are you cleared to go?"

"I'm good to go, Coach. My mother figured all that out and gave me a note two days ago."

"Is that all you have to tell me."

"No. I shot 200 foul shots since Sunday and Queens College Prep is out. I won't be competing with you in high school."

Coach Booker laughed. "If you're going to East Morris Regional you will be. Morris Brown will join the NJSIAA next year as part of its program to try to expand enrollment. We'll be in EMR's conference. I'm training somebody who may give me fits in a few years."

She bumped fists with Emily and said, "I think the choice to avoid the Queens College situation was a wise decision right now. We'll see what the future holds. See you tomorrow. Don't be late."

Emily got a surprise when she got home Her parents were flying to Pittsburgh Friday night to watch her play on Saturday. *Oh my God! Didn't Coach Booker put on enough pressure?*

CHAPTER TEN

Coach Booker brought a friend along for the trip to help with the driving and supervision. She was a big woman with brown hair cut short, who didn't bother with makeup. Her name was Margaret DiStephano. Her first words were, "I'm not going to be your buddy. Don't call me Peggy or Marge. It's either Margaret or Coach D. Got it?"

This was greeted with a chorus of "Yes, Coach."

The girls talked excitedly for a little while, but soon settled in for the long ride with their ear buds and music, or games on their cell phones. Lunch was at a rest stop on the Pennsylvania Turnpike, where Coach D organized a short exercise program to get the kinks out. She ran them around as if she were a drill sergeant, which she might have been, for all the girls knew.

They ran into a bunch of traffic as they neared Pittsburgh, so they got to the Ramada Inn later than planned. It was almost nine o'clock before they finished dinner and got to their rooms. There were four girls to a room: two to each king-sized bed. Coach Booker set lights out for ten PM and demanded they show up for breakfast by seven AM. Both Ronna and Mo were assigned to a room with Emily and Kelly, and there was quite a debate about who was going to sleep with whom.

Mo was quite explicit when she addressed Emily and Kelly, "These beds ain't near big enough for me and Ronna to sleep together. Each of you white breads is gonna have the diversity experience of your life tonight: sleepin' with a nigger. Bones, I'm gonna flip this coin. If you call it right, you get to sleep with me; wrong and Kelly has the privilege."

Emily laughed. "Do you snore?"

"My sister never complained, but then she was probably afraid to say anything. Our bed ain't as big as this one. You can tell me in the morning. . . if you got the guts. Heads or tails?"

Emily looked at Kelly, who was standing in the corner frowning. "Heads."

Mo and Emily watched as the coin spun in the air. Ronna just sat on the bed she had apparently chosen, and Kelly didn't move from her corner.

Mo said, "You win, Bones. At least you're skinnier than Kelly."

All four were quiet for a long moment as the truth of what Mo said sunk in. None of them had ever slept in the same bed with a person of another race, and Emily had never slept in a bed with anyone since she had nightmares as a kid.

Emily finally said, "They said I'd learn a lot this summer."

One of the things she learned was that the black girls slept in tee shirts and baggy gym shorts, while the white girls had cute cotton pajamas. Emily set the clock radio for six thirty.

It took a while for Emily to get to sleep. She was excited. She never thought she'd be in a hotel in Pittsburgh getting ready to play basketball before she was in high school. Gradually the rhythmic breathing of the others lulled her to sleep, and she was startled by the alarm.

Mo was already dressed in her warmup suit and pacing the width of the room. Kelly was in the bathroom and Ronna was beginning to get dressed. Mo heard the shower start and yelled, "Kelly what the hell are you doin'? We're gonna be out there sweatin' up a storm in a couple of hours. A shower now ain't gonna do you no good. Get out of there and let Bones brush her teeth."

Ronna laughed, "Captain Mo givin' orders again."

"Ain't you hungry?" snapped Mo.

Emily realized that she was hungry and barged into the bathroom. There were two sinks in there. Kelly flinched, but then shrugged, as if she'd been through this before.

They all had a big breakfast. Emily did some carbohydrate loading with pancakes. The others also did a lot of damage to the buffet. Coach D led them in a brief walk around the parking lot "to settle their stomachs", and they packed up for the short bus ride to the U. Pitt. field house.

Coach Booker was in a warmup suit and her Converse sneakers this morning, but no less focused. They found a corner to review their strategy and what little scouting information Coach had been able to dredge up roaming the halls last night. Then it was twenty minutes to nine and they were on the court warming up for the game.

Over the weeks the rotation had solidified. The starting lineup evolved to Mo, Ty, Jo, Kelly and One. If things went according to plan, the normal substitution patterns would occur. If not, Coach Booker wouldn't hesitate to shake things up. She was here to win.

With four games going on simultaneously across the main arena court there wasn't much room for spectators. The players' benches took up the room along the sides of the courts. There was space for some chairs at the ends of each court, and some folks chose to stand on the exercise track that was cantilevered off the sidewalls of the building about twelve feet over the court. John and Janet waved to Emily from a spot up there.

The referees were as fired up as the players. Coach Booker's training session paid big dividends at the start of the first game. The Mauraders got off to a fast start when a couple of their opponents got called for two early fouls each. Emily liked that. She got in earlier than normal and got some open shots because the girls guarding her were leery of collecting more fouls. It was an easy win.

Coach Booker used the time between games to deliver her "don't get a big head; remember the last time you got lazy" speech. She then relayed the input Coach D had gathered while watching their next opponent's winning effort in their first game.

They had to travel over to Robert Morris College for their second game. The set up was the same; four courts going simultaneously with little space for spectators, but parents and college scouts found places to watch the players they were interested in.

This opponent was very tall. Coach B started Mo, Ronna and Ty to balance the match ups. The game was more physical than the first one and the fouls accumulated. Emily was soon in there playing against bigger girls. She was fired up; fouls be damned, and she got called for three, but filled the minutes well, and drew some fouls on the other team's bigs with her quickness. As usual she found herself knocked to the floor more than she liked, but she scored eight points, four for four from the foul line. By the middle of the fourth quarter when Coach B put Ty and Mo back into the game, the Mauraders had a height advantage because of the disqualifications of two of the taller opponents for fouls. Mo and Ty went on a rampage under the basket. The Mauraders won by ten.

It was two PM. Their group final would be at six, back at U. Pitt., on the big court. They went back to the Ramada for a light lunch, hydration, some rest, and to let their uniforms air out and dry a little. They were to gather at the bus by five.

The brief scouting report coach D provided on their opponent was that they were "a bunch of damn water bugs"; smaller than the Mauraders, very fast, very pesky on defense, and always wanting to run.

Coach B started the usual lineup, but that didn't last long. The "water bugs" picked Ty's pocket and ran off for quick scores too often for Coach B to tolerate in the early going. She substituted Rene to cut the speed deficit. One and Two were getting run ragged on defense, so she added Emily in what amounted to a rotating three-person squad focusing on slowing the opponent's fast break. Meanwhile, when they could get the ball to Mo, she was a power underneath.

There was a lot of pressing and double-teaming of the Marauders' guards. Emily relished having a critical role by being available to receive a pass at mid court to escape the pressure. She found she could drive to the foul line, draw Mo's guard, and feed her for an easy basket underneath before the pressing guards could recover. After a couple of those, they quit pressing and switched to double teaming Mo. This left the Maurader guards with more room despite the speed of the defense. Quick ball movement set up Kelly to hit a three, Jo added one, and then was able to get a pass into Mo underneath for a layup. The life started to leak out of the legs of the water bugs. The Marauders won by a dozen.

Emily's parents insisted on taking her out for dinner after the game. Nobody objected. Everybody had some sort of celebration in mind, and they could sleep in a little tomorrow because their first game was not until eleven.

John focused on scouting and strategies for Sunday's games. Janet asked about sleeping arrangements and camaraderie, how the girls were getting along, and what Emily was finding out about her teammates. Emily answered as best she could, but a lot of it was above her pay grade. Her parents dropped her off at her hotel about 9:30 and she was ready for bed.

Her room was dark, but there was a major event going on next door. Loud laughter could be heard in the hall. She knocked on the door. A giggling Sara opened it a crack, then waved her in. Everybody was sitting on the edges of the beds. A strange odor filled the room and seemed to be emanating from a cigarette being passed from girl to girl. Each player took a puff and passed it to the next. By the time it got to Emily the butt was stuck on a tooth pick so that the last dregs of the smoke could be shared. Emily thought, *this has got to be marijuana. What the hell am I going to do?*

She was saved from that crisis by Coach D bursting into the room shouting, "What stupid shit are you jerks up to? You can smell the weed out in the hall. This place is overrun with cops for just this reason. Give me that."

She grabbed the roach from One, who had just offered it to Emily, and puffed. She savored it a moment and then said more quietly, "It's cheap shit at that. Who brought it?"

The giggling stopped. Utter silence reigned for a full minute. Coach D pinched out the last embers of the roach with her thumb and forefinger.

"I guess I didn't really expect an answer to that question, and I won't guess. I hope too many of you won't be sick tomorrow morning. This party is over. Get your asses in bed and pray that Coach B doesn't walk by this room any time soon. Breakfast is at nine."

She ushered the guests out of the room and saw to it that they went straight to their own.

As they got undressed for bed, Emily, still shaking, asked Mo, "What do you think she'll do?"

"Probably nothin'. There would have been no party if she'd been on top of things. She can't afford to turn us in. I wonder where she went tonight. Haven't seen her since dinner."

Ronna said, "She went off with a sister right after. I didn't see where they went."

"Was she another team's coach," asked Mo.

"Hell, if I know."

Mo, now playing house mother said, "All right, children brush your teeth and pack your party clothes away so there's no pot smell in this room."

Kelly laughed. "Our uniforms smell so bad nobody could smell pot anyway."

"Maybe, but tough coaches have sensitive noses," answered Mo.

They did as directed, and soon there was no sound in the room except for rhythmic breathing and an occasional snore.

They went to breakfast dressed in their warmup suits over their underwear. If they had any hopes for clean uniforms, they were dashed. Coach B wanted to stay with the lucky clothes: the soggy white/red reversible shirts and white shorts that now had a life of their own.

Their tournament semi final game was held at Robert Morris and turned out to be a laugh-er. Either their opponent had inhaled a lot more pot last night, or their group had been filled with school yard teams. Emily got to play almost half the game and scored ten points. She could almost feel her father bursting with pride up in the bleachers.

There was a pretty good crowd for the game since the losing teams from the two groups involved hung around to see who won, and a dozen more college coaches showed up to scout possible recruits. Even more scouts were expected to show up to witness the finals at two that afternoon.

Coach B had a surprise for them after the game: clean new uniforms for the final. These were the white home uniforms borrowed from the Morris Brown School for use only at a special occasion. Coach B changed her uniform too. She was once again in her designer jeans, elegant green blouse, and navy blue four-inch heels. The whole thing seemed a little like a party.

Despite Mo's cynical comment that taking a shower before playing a game was a serious waste of time, most of the girls showered before putting on the clean uniforms. They then packed up, checked out of the hotel, and gathered at the bus for the trip to the main court at the University of Pittsburgh for the final. The bus ride was quiet.

They were playing a team from Evanston, Illinois. There were perhaps a thousand spectators for the game in the cavernous U. Pitt arena. They were scattered throughout the lower stand in groups reflecting their team affiliations, including supporters of the finalists. Most of the college scouts knew each other and hung out as a group. Emily had never seen such a crowd at any game she played in, even though it filled only a small fraction of the seats in the place. She found her parents easily and waved once before focusing on her warm-ups.

At last, it was time for the introductions. As the first Maurader, Jo, was introduced, Emily noticed that the number announced was different than the number on Jo's uniform. She grabbed Coach B's arm and pointed that out. Coach went to the scorer's table. So did the lead official, a tall woman with a touch of gray at her temples. It soon became clear that all the numbers in the official score book were wrong. The official scorer had simply copied the names and numbers from the dirty shirts used in all the previous games into the book for the final game and no one had thought to check.

The lead referee shrugged and said, "Sorry, but we have to start the game with a technical foul. It wouldn't be fair to the other team to ignore the rule, and besides, the conference commissioners are watching us."

Coach B knew that, but the knowledge did nothing to calm the anger that consumed her over such a bush-league screw up. She kicked the first chair on the bench and set it flying. The action broke off the heel on the other shoe, and Coach B started an ignominious flop in front of 1000 people. Mo saved her from that at least, reacting instantly to grab her arm.

Another of the three officials appeared at her side and said, "Easy coach. Don't make it any worse than it has to be."

Coach B snapped back, "I'm not mad at you. I'm furious with myself."

"I know," the official replied, "but they don't." She waved at the spectators.

Coach B looked at the crowd and took a long breath. "I got it," she said. And gathered her team as their opponent made two foul shots to start the game with a lead.

"I'm sorry," she said. "I screwed up big time despite my efforts to get everything right. I need you to pick me up. Can you do it?"

The team shouted, "Yeah", but they knew it wouldn't be easy. While the team lined up for the jump ball, Coach B dug her sneakers out of her bag, and put them on. They destroyed her plan for an elegant appearance, but she had only herself to blame.

As the game wore on, the two points seemed insurmountable. Each time the Mauraders tied the game Evanston made a little spurt to regain the lead.

Emily got in the game for two minutes just before the end of the third quarter so that Mo could get a good rest to prepare for the final surge to the end of the game. The Mauraders were losing by two.

Emily grabbed the rebound from an opponent's shot, fired a pass to Kelly near the sideline and sprinted for their basket. Kelly passed the ball ahead to Jo who flipped it back to Emily as she raced down the foul lane toward the basket. It was the kind of play that had not happened early in the tournament season. Emily caught the ball and leaped for a layup. An opponent leaped from the side and crashed into her just as she released the try. She went flying to one side, her mouthpiece flew out as she landed on her back and slid three feet into a photographer kneeling behind the end line, smacking her mouth against his knee.

For a moment the world went round and round like a hula hoop but stabilized as she came to rest against the pudgy photographer's stomach.

Her breaths came in mighty rasps. A drip of saliva and blood ran from the corner of her mouth. She had no idea what happened to her shot, but soon found out. Kelly and Jo dragged her to her feet and pounded her back. When she caught a glimpse of the scoreboard, she saw the score was tied. It had gone in. In addition, she had a foul shot coming.

The referee said, "You have to leave the game until you get the bleeding fixed."

Coach B asked for a time out. A trainer from U. Pitt. came over and looked at her cut lip. He said, "I can stop the bleeding, but it will hurt like hell. It's the stuff professional boxers use to stop bleeding from their eyebrows. Are you game?"

"Hell yes."

He was right. The stuff he smeared on the inside of her lips did hurt like hell. Her eyes watered. The trainer put a soft roll of cotton between her teeth and lip. It felt ugly, but there was no more blood.

Coach B locked eyes with Emily and asked, "Are you OK?"

"Yeah, I guess so." She stretched both arms over her head and rotated her body from one side to the other. "All my parts seem to by be working OK."

"Can you make this foul shot?"

"Why not?"

"And I'll take care of that bitch who creamed you when I get back in there," Mo said.

Emily looked at Mo and said, "No way, Mo. You'll end up back on the bench and we'll be behind again. I'll take of things my own way." She felt a surge inside her that gave her confidence that she could do just that.

Coach B substituted Rene for Jo, and whispered instructions to her.

The referee came over and asked, "Are you OK to shoot?"

Before Coach B could open her mouth, Emily mumbled around the cotton, "Yes Ma'am. Let's go."

The buzzer sounded, and Emily made the shot with just the barest kiss on the inside of the front rim. There were 25 seconds left in the third quarter and she planned to make the most of them before she would be back on the bench.

Evanston brought the ball up the floor slowly, obviously planning to take the last shot of the period. Emily was shadowing the girl who had fouled her. Their point guard dawdled deep behind the arc killing time. Suddenly, Kelly and Rene leaped out to double-team her. She pivoted to get her back to them and attempted a pass to the girl Emily was guarding.

Mistake! Emily leaped into the space between them, intercepted the pass, and exploded toward her basket as the clock ticked off the last seconds of the quarter.

She had never dribbled so fast, nor had she felt so sure she was in control. She leaped for the basket and gently placed the ball on the backboard right at the corner of the white rectangle behind the rim. There was no doubt it would go in, nor was there any way an opponent could have caught her.

The horn to end the period sounded just as the ball hit the floor. *OK,* she thought, *I may be going back to the bench, but everybody knew I was here.* Somehow though, that was not enough now. She wanted to play more!

And she did. Mo returned, but Ronna went out, leaving an odd combination on the floor: Emily, Rene, Kelly, Mo, and Ty. It was their ball via the alternating possession procedure to start the fourth quarter. Emily could hardly stand still while Coach B told them to just play their game. Nothing special was needed now.

The teams traded baskets for a couple of minutes. Then Mo collected a long rebound, whipped it to Rene and started for the basket. Rene passed ahead to Emily in the corner who bounced the ball to Mo barreling down the lane. Mo slammed on the brakes and spun away from Emily. Emily knew Mo was going to shoot no matter what her defender did. She brushed past the girl guarding her and sprinted toward the hoop. Mo flipped up a soft jump-hook just over the reach of her defender. It bounced off the rim on Emily's side. Emily leaped for the rebound transferring all her momentum into vertical energy. She snatched the ball from the big girl who was recovering from contesting Mo's shot and put it back into the basket just before getting clobbered once again.

Mo dragged Emily from the floor in the quiet moment after the whistle blew for the foul. She said, "Way to pick me up, Bones."

Emily smiled, her heart still racing. The racing heart did not interfere with her making the foul shot. The Mauraders were ahead by four.

Coach B shifted them into a 1-3-1 zone defense with Emily at the point near the division line. If the ball got past Emily, the idea was for her to turn back and double-team the ball with whoever was guarding the girl holding it. Sometimes that forced a turnover; sometimes that girl managed to get a pass to a teammate near the endline where there was only Mo or Ty to guard two opponents. The strategy resulted in a trade off.

During one such double-team the ball came loose. Emily dove for it, grabbed it and slid several feet on her chest. As her slide came to an end, she rolled the ball toward Kelly, who grabbed it and started the other way. While fans screamed for a traveling violation, Kelly passed to Rene, who made a layup. The Mauraders were up by six. Emily had the wind knocked out of her.

One replaced her. Coach B gave her a high five, and she collapsed on the bench. The trainer came and replaced the roll of cotton in her mouth with a fresh one.

The six-point lead was short-lived. On their next possession Evanston stuck a three. Rene got carried away and tried to retaliate with an off-balance heave. Not good. Less than a minute later Evanston got the ball into the pivot where their player made a short jumper to cut the lead to one. Coach B asked for a time out. Emily bounced off her chair to join the huddle.

Coach B said, "Alright, if we can hold on to this lead for a minute and a half, we get the trophy. They're going to press like demons and foul us every time we get the ball. We gotta take care of the ball and make our foul shots. Jo you're in for Rene. What about you, Bones? Have you still got the rhythm at the foul line?"

Emily blurted out, "Coach I'm ready for anything."

Coach B studied her for a few seconds, then said, "OK. You're in for One. Mo, Ty on the press-break make yourself available for the release pass in center court if the guards get jammed up but get the ball back to a guard as soon as you can. Everybody got it?" They just nodded. They had work to do.

Evanston pressed on the throw-in but did not foul when Jo got the ball to Kelly. They were content to get the ball back with about a minute left after the Mauraders ran out the shot clock. The Mauraders ran their high post offense for 25 seconds, but Kelly missed a three. At the other end Emily's girl posted her up on the blocks. *They think they can take advantage of me* she realized. *It ain't gonna happen.*

She got her arm around in front of the girl to prevent a pass. The girl drove an elbow into her chest, driving her back a step. Emily saw red when there was no whistle. She leaped back and got a hand on the pass, knocking it to the floor. A scrum for possession of the ball followed. The referee called a jump ball. Evanston had the arrow throw-in at the end line, with 40 seconds left in the game and 10 on the shot clock.

Evanston tried to run their biggest girl down the lane for a lob pass, but Ty cut her off. The throw-in then went outside to their best long-range shooter with Jo in her face. Two dribbles later she launched a desperation try which hit the front rim and bounced to Mo. As Evanston charged her to foul, she whipped the ball to Emily, who started up the court.

The pursuit caught up with Emily near the division line and pushed her in the back, causing her to stumble.

"That's intentional," screamed Coach B.

The foul was obviously intentional, but it was not what NCAA officials wanted to call "Flagrant 1", which would involve a penalty of two shots and a throw-in. It was the ninth team foul by Evanston, so they awarded her a one and one bonus penalty. If she made the first shot, she would get a second.

All the Mauraders held their breath except Emily. The subs linked their arms on the bench and bowed their heads as if in prayer.

Emily saw the world and the basket very clearly. She accepted the pass from the official, bounced the ball a couple of times as she normally did and sank the first shot cleanly. As the referee bounced the ball to her for the second shot, the Evanston coach asked for time out.

Coach B discussed two scenarios in the huddle: one if Emily made the shot, the other if she didn't. Emily didn't listen to the second option.

When they were all lined up on the lane again, and the referee was about to bounce the ball to Emily, the Evanston coach asked for another time out, her last.

That really pissed Emily off. *Do I look like that much of a wimp?* she thought. *I'll show that jerk.*

They went through the routine at the huddle again. This time Coach B added a reminder that they a time out left as they broke to return to play.

It would have been more dramatic if Emily had missed the shot, or if the ball had hit the rim and bounced around a bit before going in, but that's not what happened. It was nothing but nylon for a three-point lead.

"Guard the arc," shouted coach B as they hustled backup the court. Emily found a second to point her forefinger at the Evanston coach, who voiced a profanity in return.

They were going to play man-to-man defense with Jo on Evanston's best three-point shooter. Evanston whipped the ball around outside the arc with their big girls trying to set a screen for a three-point shot. Ty hedged out on those screens and Jo fought around them to take the three away. As time was running out the girl chose to drive to the basket hoping to make a layup and get fouled.

"Let her go," screamed Coach B, and they heard her. She made the layup uncontested with 10 seconds left in the game. Since the clock stops on a basket in the last minute there was no rush to get the throw-in made. The Mauraders set up one of their new inbounds plays. They got the ball to Mo over a screen by Jo. Mo got rid of the ball faster than she had hidden the rest of the weed last night when Coach D broke into their little party. She threw it to Emily who wrapped both arms around it and awaited the Evanston attack. She was fouled with five seconds left.

This time she got two shots because it was the tenth foul. Coach B ordered all the rest of the team into the defensive end of the court. Emily made the first one as smoothly as she had the others. Jo ran over to her then and said, "Coach said to miss this one on purpose, but remember to hit the rim. Can you do that?"

Emily thought about that for the few seconds she had and decided she could. She lined up two inches further back from the foul line than normal but went through her normal shooting routine. The shot hit the front of the rim and fell straight down. The two Evanston players in the nearest lane spaces both grabbed for the ball, the clock started, one of them tried to throw the ball to their three-point shooter near midcourt, but Mo was there to intercept, and the game was over. The 200 practice foul shots Emily had taken during the past week had paid off.

Of course, John Barker was beside himself with joy and pride. Even Janet seemed excited. She gave her sweaty daughter a big hug. "You were David among all those Goliaths. I'm really proud of you," she said. "You can do anything you put that mind to."

"OK, Mom, OK. Enough Don't let Dad demand too many pictures, please. That would not be cool. We have some celebrating to do."

That scared Janet a little. She didn't know what kind of celebrating 16-year-old girls did.

After the high fives, the hugs, the trophy presentation, and the showers, Coach B collected the team and hustled them onto the bus for the long ride home. The girls started off the trip pretty hyper but fell asleep after they ate. It was almost midnight when they got home, but Coach B took the time to collect the uniform from each player and gave each one a hug. "It's been a great season," she said. "I hope some of you will be back next spring. I know you'll all have a great season on your school teams this winter. I might see some of you play in my travels."

They all hugged and headed to the waiting cars for the return to normal life.

CHAPTER ELEVEN

Emily slept in the next morning, then she started with the text messages to her girl friends. By the time she got downstairs it was ten o'clock. Her mother was making out a food shopping list at the kitchen table. "Made you some pancakes," she said, "but you'll have to warm them up in the nuke."

"Pancakes are good," she said, "and now that it's really summer, I need a new bathing suit."

"Doesn't last year's suit still fit?"

"Mom, I've grown two inches since last summer, besides it's way out of style."

"What does that mean?"

"Caitlin and Suzy have bikinis."

"I'm not sure that will work with your father---or me either, though our reasons may be different."

"What's Dad got against bikinis?"

"It's more about letting go for him. Let's save that fight for when it's really important. I don't think you would look good in a bikini."

"Mom, I can't be like a nerd, you know. It's not only for the town pool. There'll be parties at friends' pools too."

Janet laughed. "Do you girls ever actually go in the water?"

"Yes, we do. Besides, looking good outside the pool is important."

"Ems, I don't think you have developed enough to look good in a bikini. You may look like an elongated fifth grader."

"Mom!"

"Tell you what: let's see what we can find on the internet."

They sat together on the couch and cranked up Janet's laptop. It turned out to be true that the models who looked good and comfortable in bikinis had a lot more boob and more butt than Emily had at this point in her life.

"Do you think I could pad the bra?" asked Emily.

"And what would happen if you actually got thrown into the pool?"

"Damn."

"Ems, is that language something you learned on the AAU basketball circuit?"

"No, Mom. A lot of my friends from school use four letter words."

"Not in front of me or your father they don't."

"I get the message. Sorry, but let's get back to bathing suits."

"What about a one-piece suit like the Olympic swimmers wore? Most of them were flat-chested but looked good and had some style."

"I don't know."

Janet tapped on some keys and another set of models appeared. Two of those were members of the Olympic team. Janet noted that the official Olympic suits cost fifty percent more than those that were only of a similar style.

"What do you think about something like these?"

Emily sighed. "They look OK, but that's probably because the girls wearing them are champions."

"You're a champion too."

"Nice try, Mom."

"You are a champ, Ems. Never forget that. Tell you what. Suppose we send some of these pictures to Caitlin and Suzy and see what their reaction is."

Emily thought for a moment. *Maybe the girls would be happy to see her in a yucky suit this summer to give them an edge with the boys. Nah. They were her friends.* "OK let's see what they say, but I'm not making any commitments yet."

"Fair enough. Give me their phone numbers."

"Suppose you just ship the pictures to my phone, and I'll stick a note on top of them and send them to Caitlin and Suzy."

Janet said, "Well OK," and went about the transfer.

It took only a few minutes to compose the question and transmit half-dozen pictures to the girls.

The feedback didn't take long in coming either. Caitlin pointed out that they cost a lot more than her bikini had but looked OK. Suzy thought the one-piece suits didn't look nearly as sophisticated as they should for a high school girl.

Janet said, "A split vote. Does that leave me with the tie breaker?"

"OK, Mom. Are you sure you want to spend the extra money?"

"We spend money for value, Ems. You get what you pay for if you know what you're doing."

"Yeah, Mom. You tell me that at least once a month."

Janet had to smile at that. Then she had a sobering thought. "Is sophisticated a euphemism for sexy or hot with girls these days?"

"I don't know. Suzy is pretty much into looking good for the boys I guess."

"Do you know whether she fools around with *Kik* or *After School*, or another of those apps that flirt with sex and abuse?"

"I don't know anything about *Kik*, but I've heard some stuff about *After School*. Kids can say nasty things about other kids without giving their names. It can get ugly. Somebody said a 15-year-old girl committed suicide somewhere over the abuse she got. Who would want to mess with that stuff?"

"Ems, will you promise me to let me know if you find out that any of your friends do mess with that stuff?"

"I can't control what they do, Mom, but I'm not gonna fool with it. Can we get back to the bathing suit?"

"Emily, I want you to look good all the time, like an intelligent young lady, like a young lady who's confident in her own skin. You are who you are, not some would-be Barbie doll. I have the addresses of a couple of local stores that sell the Olympic style suits. Let's go see what we can find."

Emily was quiet for a moment then said, "Whatever, but I have the right of approval."

"Of course. Let me make a quick call and we're off. If we're successful we'll have lunch some place nice."

Emily didn't hear all her mother's side of her phone conversation, but it seemed she was canceling an appointment for the afternoon. Emily wondered what that was about for a minute, but then put her mind back on the bathing suit problem. *What if she was the only girl in her group not wearing a bikini this summer?*

They went to two big sporting goods stores without success. They had swim team suits that were either all labeled with team names or plain black. At a small store in Chatham, they found something worth trying on. The sales lady was an older woman who was delighted to help. Emily had to admit she liked how she looked in a couple of the suits. She looked lean, but not skinny, and there was a little padding in the top of one model.

Her mother seemed willing to spend the extra money for the official Olympic model, but Emily liked the one with the padding better. The sales lady agreed; didn't seem at all interested in the extra sales bucks. The deal was done, a navy-blue suit with shoulder straps and a red and white stripe under each arm. They all felt good.

It was two o'clock before they got to lunch at Panera, where they indulged in a cup of potato soup and half a chicken sandwich. They talked of other preparations for the start of high school and possibilities for the course electives Emily would be able to choose.

Emily felt it was a great day; a wonderful start to a summer she had great plans for.

One of those plans was to begin working with some of the weights her father kept in the basement and used about once a week. She had learned from her AAU experience that she could benefit from adding some upper body muscle in the rebound scrums. She also wanted to increase her jumping ability for the same reason. She had been doing some research on the internet for the appropriate exercises. She started by jumping onto the second step of the porch stairs. In a few days she realized that was too easy, so she switched to the seat of the living room couch. That didn't fly with Mom. Her father built her a sturdy box two feet high to work on, and she worked.

She also devised a plan to add some beef to her bones in preparation for her first high school season. Billy Pedrazi had suggested adding protein shakes to her diet, as he was doing. Emily got a big plastic can of vanilla flavored pure whey protein; and mixed it with milk. She drank one of these concoctions after every workout.

Her plans to hang out at the town pool every day got abridged a little by a baby-sitting job, but it was fun to chase a two-year old around the big back yard of a neighbor's house.

Teen nights at the town pool were a lot of fun. The management of the pool closed it early every other Saturday and then reopened at eight for teenagers only. Caitlin, Suzy, and a few other girls in their class generally came, as did Billy Pedrazi, Ralph Steele, Bobby Martin and some the other boys who used to come to watch the basketball and softball games. Older teens, those with access to a car, found other things to do on Saturday nights, so freshmen and sophomores were the big shots at the gathering.

There were many things to do at these events. A variety of water games and swimming races were offered; there was a volleyball pitch, and a small basketball court. Rock and roll music and related genres blasted loud enough for the neighbors to complain, and some kids danced along the pool deck until some wise guy started to push people into the water. Pizza from the concession stand was the food of choice.

And while they ate, they talked. Those about to enter high school were particularly excited, and full of what they would achieve. They were also blossoming physically and socially. While Emily hadn't gotten there yet, she did see some stuff going on. Suzy and Caitlin contrived to sit next to Bill Pedrazi whenever possible. Suzy even punched him lightly on the arm to emphasize a joke and did other stuff Emily thought was stupid. Ralph and Bobby tried to horn in on a slice of all this camaraderie whenever they could. *Is that what bikinis did to kids?* wondered Emily.

Billy stood over six feet tall and was focused on playing basketball. He had been Emily's peer as the star of the Ridge boys' team. He was a good-looking young man, his light brown hair flecked with blond highlights from the sun, there was a little tuft of hair growing on his tanned chest, but his cheeks still had a boyish blush.

He seemed more interested in Emily's AAU experience than in the attentions of either Suzy or Caitlin. She felt uneasy about having private conversations with Billy because of Caitlin and Suzy's obvious interest in him. She usually found a way to draw them into any conversation. As it turned out there was a lot of interest in a few of her stories, especially those from the trip to Pittsburgh.

The girls were shaken by thoughts of sleeping in the same bed with anyone, let alone a giant black girl from Newark.

"They were just players," asserted Emily. "We played against a lot of black girls in the tournaments. We just played. The game was what it was all about."

"Did they smell?" asked Suzy.

Emily laughed. "We all smelled. We played two or three games a day in boiling hot gyms, and our uniforms were soaked in sweat by the end of the first half of the first game. It didn't matter."

By then the girls were holding their noses, but they stayed to listen more.

The idea of playing in smelly uniforms and not taking a shower every morning caused groans, but the real spellbinder was the story of walking in on the pot party. Emily swore them all to silence before she told that one. The reactions to the story ranged from Suzy and Bobby's excitement to horror on the part of others. Emily was sure the story would get spread all over the class before long. She felt confident that no one would tell their parents but couldn't be sure. She decided she had better fill her mother in on all the details just in case.

Not to be outdone, Suzy took the floor. "You know my sister, Dorothy, graduated from high school this June. She said that there were a few kids into pot in her class, but most of the class went to the all-night graduation party at Playtown. She said the place was overrun with parents and there were even two cops there, so nothing bad happened. The kids swam and danced like we do here, and there were a ton of games to play. Lots of food too."

One of the listeners asked, "Does everybody really go to that party?"

"Pretty much. You know that a bunch of parents started the thing a long time ago after four graduates got drunk at a graduation party and drove their car into a tree, killing the whole bunch. Now the real parties come after graduation. The best ones happen at people's houses down at the shore, but my parents had one up here."

"What was that like?" asked Bobby. "Did they let you go?"

"Of course. There were some of my parent's friends there too."

"Sounds dull," said Bobby, and the group laughed.

"Not really. Some of the kids got into the beer. My father went around and collected everybody's car keys; wouldn't let some guys drive home, or anywhere for that matter. That caused some screaming and yelling. He ended up driving two kids home, which got them in a bunch of trouble. Dorothy had to listen to a lot of abuse about our parents at a couple of later parties."

Emily wondered what her parents would do if they ever had a graduation party. She knew that when they graduated from high school in New York, the drinking age was only 18. She'd heard her father say that if a kid was old enough to vote or get shot at in the army, they ought to be able to drink. Still, the law was now 21 everywhere thanks to the Federal Government.

That night Caitlin called Emily after she had gone to bed. She thought maybe something terrible had happened, but Caitlin's first words were, "Do you like Billy Pedrazi?"

"Huh? What's that all about?"

"You spent most of the night talking to him."

"We were talking about protein shakes and getting ready for freshman basketball."

"Ems, sometimes you're so oblivious. Do you LIKE him? Do you want him to hold your hand?"

"That's yucky, Caitlin. Who wants to do that?"

"I do, and so does Suzy. I think she went over the top tonight punching him on the arm and squeezing in next to him on the bench."

"I saw that. Suzy is just . . . I don't know . . . dramatic."

"And I'm not. Will you whisper in her ear to calm down?"

"Caitlin, you're my friend. So is Suzy. I'm not going to get involved in your fight over who is going to sit next to Billy Pedrazi."

Caitlin shouted into the phone, "Thanks a lot, Emily. Some friend you are."

Emily said, "Caitlin, wait I . . ." then she realized that Caitlin had hung up on her.

Emily lay there looking at her phone for a minute, then turned it off. *What was going to happen now?*

- - - - - -

Another big event of the summer was the orientation day for freshmen at the high school. An orientation was needed because East Morris Regional was not a typical high school. The campus consisted of six buildings connected by covered walkways. The main building contained the auditorium, cafeteria, a gathering space, and offices. The gym, classrooms and laboratories were all located in the outlying buildings. Without a map and a tour, freshmen often got lost.

Seniors guided groups of incoming students to each of the buildings and offered comments about what to wear in bad weather, and absolute prohibitions about getting off the paved paths and wearing out the grass spaces. Emily and her gang had a great time razzing each other about who would get lost first, and who would avoid classes located in the farthest building.

Signing up for their class schedule was another chore for orientation day. The base curriculum was full of requirements for most students: Algebra II, Language arts, Biology, Social Science, Health/Phys Ed., and two electives. One of those was almost always a language, which left one freebie. A few students had special needs, and those were shuttled off to the guidance office as soon as the issue came up. Emily chose Spanish and Choir and was glad to see that Billy Pedrazi was in her Algebra II section. He was a whiz at math, and she might need help. Some of her buddies were in some of her other class sections, but there was no class where all of them were together. The school wanted to promote mixing of the teens from the two towns that constituted the district. The goal was forming a cohesive student body. Emily decided it was a good day. Another hurdle gotten over.

All this went on in the absence of basketball---almost. Emily ran three miles four or five days a week, took 100 foul shots each week, and worked her foot work with her father a couple of evenings a week. Shooting practice was unscheduled but happened for a few minutes most days. Mostly she worked on the weights in the basement and jumping up on the box her father made. She kept up with the protein shakes. With encouragement from her mother, she also let her hair grow. Now it went into a short ponytail which she thought made her look a little more grownup.

The family had a week's vacation at the shore the last week in August, which included Emily's fourteenth birthday. They rented a small house two blocks off the beach in Manasquan. The weather was great that week. Emily substituted swimming for her runs but had brought her weights with her on the trip. She and her parents ate out several times, and just hung out. Her parents did have the restaurant provide a tiny birthday cake, which embarrassed Ems no end. She enjoyed being part of adult conversations, except those involving politics. She was glad to have brought some DVDs with her. Regular TV was saturated with pompous blowhards telling the masses how they would get make life better for everybody if they got elected.

There was still Labor Day weekend to celebrate before starting school. Suzy's parents decided to have a party at their house in Ocean Grove and invite some of Suzy's friends. Dorothy was leaving for college in North Carolina the day after the holiday, so it was like a rite of passage: one daughter finished with high school and moving on; and her sister moving in to fill the void.

The original plan was for Dorothy to drive the kids down in the family van, her parents right behind in a separate car on Friday about noon. Unfortunately, Mr. Highland had an emergency at work and could not take Friday off. Mrs. Highland suggested they send Dorothy and the freshmen down on schedule and follow with her husband either that night or early Saturday morning. She felt comfortable in having Dorothy supervise her sister and four friends: Emily, Caitlin, Billy, and Ralph. Janet was not at all comfortable. She called Mrs. Highland Thursday after Emily reported the change of plans.

"I've heard some scary stories about shore weekends. Tell me exactly what will be going on."

"They'll get down there in time for a swim in the afternoon Friday, Dorothy will get them pizza for supper, and then I guess they'll go for a walk on the boardwalk until dark or so. Ocean Grove is a quiet town with a great beach."

"Are you sure Dorothy is ready to watch over five 14-year-olds?"

"Oh, my yes. She has been babysitting since she was Suzy's age. Lately she has people hire her when they're going to be away overnight. She's very reliable."

Janet said no more but had some misgivings about what John might think when he got home that night.

When John heard the story at dinner, he said very simply, "You're not going there tomorrow."

"Dad!"

"That's final," said her father. "I may be forty-five years old, but I can still remember what it was like to be eighteen and full of macho hormones."

Janet said, "John, these kids are only fourteen. You've met them all at basketball games. Didn't they seem nice?"

"Of course, they did. I'm much more concerned about how they behave after they have a couple of beers in them."

"Who said anything about beer?" snapped Emily as her face scrunched up and she struggled to hold back her tears.

"That's the problem," replied her father. "Nobody ever says anything about beer, but it always shows up. Some would-be stud has an older brother or bribes a guy to get it for him. You know what can happen at drunken parties. As big as you are, you'll be the baby in the group. I'm not about to let you take that kind of risk. You aren't going to any shore house unless there are parents there."

Emily's eyes overflowed. "Dad, I'll be the laughingstock of my friends."

"You'll be a safe laughingstock. That's all I care about."

Emily screamed, "You're horrible!" With that, she leaped up, ran for the stairs, and slammed the door to her bedroom, the vibrations of which shook the walls in the kitchen.

John looked at his wife, his chin thrust forward.

She said, "I guess I shouldn't have called you at the office. Maybe you wouldn't have come home so loaded for bear. You know you can't even buy beer in Ocean Grove."

"Jan, they can buy it right across the street in Asbury Park. Are you willing to take that risk? She's just a kid. There are too many for one 18-year-old to watch over. And they'll be out on the board walk at night."

"In many ways she's a precocious kid."

"With a basketball, yeah, but that also means she's naive in other ways."

"Maybe you underestimate her, John. She's been running around with older kids most of her life."

"She isn't going to the shore," he said, turned on his heel and headed for the TV.

Janet brewed herself a cup of tea and thought about the situation. She wanted Emily to have a normal social life but had to admit that being invited to a shore house for even one night without parents there scared her too.

In time she got up and cleaned the dishes from the table. *So little had been eaten on what could have been a joyous evening,* she thought. She scraped the food into the garbage and loaded the dishes into the dish washer. Then she sighed and headed upstairs to Emily's room.

She knocked on the door. "It's Mom, Emily. Open up."

"I don't want to talk."

"You're going to have to, if we're ever going to fix this situation."

"How are we going fix anything? He's got his chin stuck out like when he's trying to fix something himself and won't call a repair man."

Janet laughed. "It's a little like that, but I've lived with him for twenty years, and there's always some hope."

There was silence for over a minute and then she heard the lock click. The door opened to reveal Emily, her eyes swollen, her cheeks still wet, and her body sagging. Her mother took her in her arms and patted her back as she had done to get her to burp fourteen years ago. Then she said, "Let's do a little brainstorming."

"Your father is afraid for your safety, Ems. You can't blame him for that."

"He thinks I'm still a baby."

"Not really, but it is hard for him to loosen the strings on his only sweet daughter. Let me tell you a story."

They sat side-by-side on the bed.

"You knew I grew up in Manhattan, right. Met your father at Manhattan College where he played basketball. My family had a few bucks. I went to private school and hung out with people who also went to private schools and had a few bucks. In those days senior proms were big events, almost like a debutante cotillion.

"The school I went to held the dance in the gym, but afterward we went to a small night club where one of the fathers paid the head waiter to ignore drinking rules, but also to watch over us kids to see nobody got seriously drunk. That was fine, but there was an after party at the executive suite in a nice hotel to which a father had access. There was no watchdog there. A couple of really bad things happened to two of my girlfriends. I'll never forget those, or the fact that the boys who did them were our friends."

"What kind of things happened, Mom?"

"I'm not going to discuss the details. They were stupid and ugly, and destroyed friendships for the rest of the people's lives. Do you want to take a chance on that?"

Emily wrapped her arms across her chest, looked at the floor, and was quiet for a long moment. Janet wondered what pictures were flipping through her daughter's mind but said nothing until Emily looked back at her.

"To me the lesson is that kids need watchdogs at such parties even at fourteen. How can we arrange that at the Highland shore house tomorrow night?"

"I don't know, Mom."

"Will Billy sign on as your guardian angel in front of your father?"

"You know, outside of basketball, I really don't know him very well. I'd bet that making anybody go face-to-face with Daddy right now is not going to work."

Jan smiled. "Now that I think about that, you're probably right. I've met Mrs. Pedrazi a couple of times. May I talk to her about the shore house?"

Emily just shrugged. Her mother said, "Do you have their home number?"

Emily scrolled through the contacts on her cell phone and showed the number to her mother.

Jan dialed it and caught Louise Pedrazi in her kitchen. "Hello, Mrs. Pedrazi, this is Janet Barker. I hope I didn't catch you at a bad time."

After a moment of silence, she went on, "thank you Louise, we've been talking with Emily about the plans for the weekend and had a few questions."

Emily could only guess what was being said on the other end of the line from her mother's cryptic comments between silences.

"Are you really comfortable letting Billy go to the Highland shore house with no parent there tomorrow night?"

"It's good to know cell coverage is excellent there, but if there were to be a problem, they would have to call the local police, or God forbid, a local ambulance."

"Yes, I agree that Billy is a great young man. If he made a promise to me, I'd believe that he would keep it. That gives me an idea. Would he promise me to act as guardian angel for Emily no matter what anybody else does?"

""That's very kind of you, Louise. I think we can do that over the phone."

"Billy, your mother already told you what this is about. I know it's strange, but will you promise me that you will see to it that nothing foolish involving you and Emily will go on at the shore house tomorrow night? I need to have a bodyguard for her, or her father won't let her go."

"You are a remarkable young man, Billy. I'm sure your parents are very proud of you, and of course, Emily will be telling the world about how you saved the day. Thank you."

"You'd rather Emily not say anything to anybody?"

"OK. You're in charge."

She hung up and smiled at Emily. "That's the kind of young man your father might approve dating his daughter. Leave this to me. Wipe your eyes and get to sleep."

The next morning Emily got up very early so she could apologize to her father before he left for work. When she got to the kitchen she was greeted with the aroma of freshly brewed coffee. Her parents sat there each sipping a steaming mug. They looked relaxed.

She said, "I'm sorry I had a melt-down last night, Dad. I didn't mean what I said."

He said, "I knew that Ems. I know I sounded like the Grinch. I appreciate your getting up early to see me off, but I suspect you knew your mother was going to get me to change my mind."

"What! I don't know anything about that."

John put his coffee cup down on the kitchen counter and took his daughter in his arms. "You know that I'm just concerned about your safety, Right? I suspect there will be more situations like last night in our future. It's hard for this old man to let go, but your mother has talked me into letting Billy Pedrazi stand in for me tonight. You made me promise to keep my mouth shut at your basketball games. Will you promise to avoid anything that's not safe this weekend?"

"Of course," said Emily trying not to bounce up and down.

"Then go and enjoy it."

Emily looked at her mother who smiled over her coffee cup. Emily buried her head against her father's chest. "Thanks, Dad," she said. "I'll try to be calmer the next time."

John scowled. "There had better not be a next time." Then he winked and both her parents smiled. "Gotta' go. Have a nice weekend."

Emily let go of her father and said, "Thanks a lot you guys."

When her father was out the door, Emily said, "Mom. I don't know how you did that, but I really appreciate it. What are you guys going to do this weekend?"

"We might take a ride to the shore one day."

Emily looked at the ceiling, shook her head, and headed upstairs. She felt the need for communication with her friends.

— — — — — —

The trip to Ocean Grove went smoothly. Dorothy was a careful driver, and the traffic wasn't too bad. They argued about what kind of tunes to play on the sound system and reached a practical compromise: Dorothy was the driver, and her word was law, so they had to listen to "The Boss", Bruce Springsteen. Dorothy had no interest in what she called "those kiddie bands" the younger passengers in her car shouted for.

They unloaded their stuff at the house. It was quite a place, an old stone building three stories high. Houses like it on the beach road had been converted to bed and breakfast establishments charging a pretty penny during the season. This house had six bedrooms but only two bathrooms. The first floor had an updated kitchen next to a dining room with a table for twelve on one side of a central hall. The other side consisted of a single large room with a real fireplace. Emily, used to a classic split-level house, was amazed. Equally amazing was the porch that ran across the south-facing front of the house and wrapped around to cover part of the west side, where the driveway was located.

They quickly dumped their stuff in the bedrooms Suzy assigned them and hiked the two blocks over to the beach carrying blankets and an umbrella from the house. There they found the daily beach fee was eight dollars, but Suzy had six season passes. She said, "When my parents get here, we're going to have to take turns buying passes, because we won't have enough."

The beach was half full and the sun-lit sand burned their feet as they worked their way to a space near the water big enough to accommodate the group. The ocean was just the right temperature to be both welcoming and refreshing. The waves were rather rough, though. Emily was glad she was not wearing a bikini. Her friends were having trouble keeping their tops in place when they got bounced around by the surf.

Billy and Ralph showed off their body-surfing skills, challenging each other to see who got the best ride. Emily thought it looked like great fun to come flying toward the beach on top of a wave with their heads out of the crest. Fun until the wave broke at the shore and dropped them out into a few inches of receding water which barely covered the pebbles and bits of shell that cycled a few feet out and back at the edge of the water with each wave. When they finally ran out of gas, their chests bore some stripes from those encounters.

It was a great afternoon. They spent all their energy and were grateful to lie on the blankets and doze off for a bit before packing up and heading back to the house.

After some negotiation they allocated the bathrooms by gender, showered, and changed. True to Mrs. Highland's agenda, Dorothy ordered pizza and sodas for dinner. Dorothy seemed to know the delivery boy. They sat on the porch and ate amid raucous retellings of the afternoon's adventures with the surf.

The girls cleaned up the mess while Dorothy took a call from her parents. The boys just sat there. Emily thought, *they have already assumed a macho attitude about housework*.

Dorothy announced, "Mom and Dad won't be coming until tomorrow. Dad is still at the office."

Emily looked at Billy, who just smiled and gave her a "thumbs up".

Suzy said, "Let's go check out the board walk."

This was greeted with approval by the freshmen, but Dorothy demurred. "I'll just relax here. Behave yourselves."

They set out north along the wide planks that bordered the beach just as the sun was setting. They had the wits to bring a light jacket or sweater in anticipation of a chill after dark. Unless one was interested in studying the architecture of the large B&Bs along Ocean Drive or the other hikers and bike riders that populated the broad path, there was little to see in Ocean Grove.

Billy and Emily brought up the rear of the squad talking about their hope for success in basketball in high school and beyond.

Emily said, "Ever since I got that scholarship offer from prep school, my father has talking about getting a scholarship to play in college. Does your father talk like that?"

"You know," he said, "only about two percent of male high school basketball players make their college teams. Girls are about twice as likely to make it. The trick is to play lacrosse."

"Where did you get all those numbers?"

"Just my mathematical bent, I guess, but my father had some input."

"How so?"

"He was a very good baseball player in high school. He went to St. Matthew's Prep in West Orange. St. Matts they called it. A thousand boys still go there, and they still win a lot of state championships in a lot of sports."

"Sure. A few of the kids we graduated with are going there."

"My father was a regular in the St. Matts lineup from the start of his junior year and had a career batting average over 400 on a state championship team."

"More numbers," said Emily.

"Yeah, but these were important. He got drafted by the St. Louis Cardinals when he graduated. They offered him a bonus of $2,000 to sign. His father said no to that. His son was going to college, the first one in the family. When it became clear that he wouldn't sign, the scout called a former teammate of his who coached at the University of North Carolina. That guy offered my father a partial scholarship and a job parking cars and cleaning out the stadium for football games. Grandpa gave his blessing, and my dad went south."

The group stopped for a brief rest at the gazebo on the boardwalk that the town and some of its churches used for gatherings. Caitlin joined them. Emily said, "I bet I can jump up on this bench from a standing start."

"You're kidding," said Billy.

"Absolutely not. If I do it and you can't, you have to carry my chair to the beach tomorrow." She did not tell him that her father had twice added height to the box she had been jumping on, and now it was up to three feet high.

"OK. You're on."

She got up, stood facing the bench and jumped up, landing in perfect balance on the seat.

Billy said, "Well if you can, so can I."

But he couldn't. He almost got there but kept getting only his toes on the seat and falling back off. After three tries he threw his hands up in surrender. "I'll have to work on this," he said.

Emily laughed. "Catch me if you can," she said.

Suzy confronted them. "What are you doing?"

"Just comparing hops," said Emily.

"Is basketball all you can think about?" She had a huge grin on her face. It seemed to light up the shadows in the gazebo, almost as if it were Christmas morning. Caitlin was grinning too.

"Come on, you guys. We're going to explore Asbury Park."

"Isn't that a little far to go?" asked Emily.

"Nah," answered Suzy. "It's right up there. You can see the lights from here."

They got up and trailed along as before. Emily wanted to know more about Billy's father and his college career. "How did it go in North Carolina?"

"Great for a while. He got to play some as a freshman, and was a regular as a soph. As he tells it, he began to realize that athletes at UNC lived a very segregated life; not racially, but socially. They were working on their sport all year. They had to avoid afternoon classes to be able to practice and play during the season and in the fall too. While some of the basketball players came from the north, most of the baseball players came from what he called the tobacco farms. It also became clear that he had no major field of study. He transferred to Adelphi on Long Island at the start of his third year."

"Well, it took him three more years to get enough credits for a degree in Education. He had only two years of college eligibility left and was still hitting the hell out of the ball. But Adelphi was small time compared to UNC, so the pro scouts didn't go by very often."

"So, a sad ending to a college scholarship athlete's career?"

"No. He got a job teaching at Madison high school and soon was coaching the baseball team. I think it will be twenty years next year. It's all good."

"The more I learn about where our parents came from, the more amazed I get," said Emily. "And you never played baseball?"

Billy burst out laughing. "Ems, from either side of the plate, I made you look like Babe Ruth. My old man didn't know much about basketball, but he could sure tell the difference between me with a bat in my hand and a baseball player. He learned about baskets in a hurry."

As they approached fancy arch that marked the beginning of Asbury Park, Suzy screamed, "There it is."

"There what is?" asked Billy.

"The Stone Pony. That's where Bruce Springsteen started. Let's go see if he's going to be there tonight."

Caitlin said, "Come on, Suzy. He's probably out on tour someplace."

Ralph said, "I heard he sometimes stops by for a surprise."

"Come on," shouted Suzy. She climbed down the steps from the boardwalk to the street and started to run down the block toward the low-slung beige stucco building with the brown roof on the next corner. After looking at each other for a moment, the group started after her much more slowly.

A very large man was smiling at Suzy when the rest arrived at the door to the place. "The Boss is not expected tonight." Then he pointed to a sign next to the door. It said, "You must have two forms of ID showing you are 21 to enter, and there's a $10 cover charge."

The big guy said, "Thanks for stopping by kids. Come back again in what, ten years?" He was still smiling.

Caitlin burst out laughing

Suzy wilted in the face of this development. "Let's head home. It's getting late."

They climbed back up on the boardwalk and headed south. They didn't talk much on the walk back to the house. Fatigue was beginning to take its toll. There was a surprise when they got there though: Dorothy had friends visiting.

Two guys and a girl from her class sat on the porch with her, beers in hand. Dorothy frowned at their arrival. The freshmen went around to the side porch to contemplate the situation. Suzy came a couple of steps behind with a beer in her hand.

She took a sip and said, "Who is up to try some beer?" She held the bottle out to Billy.

He said, "No thanks."

Ralph saw a chance to be macho and reached for the bottle. Suzy hesitated, as if she wouldn't be satisfied unless Billy put his lips where her's had been, but then handed the bottle to Ralph. With all eyes on him he took a sip, made a face, and passed the bottle to Caitlin. She just offered the bottle to Emily. Emily, remembering her father's fears, backed away in her chair. Billy stood up, took the bottle, and gave it back to Suzy. He asked, "Dorothy give you this to make sure you don't spill the beans on her?"

Suzy's face dropped. "We can't tell my parents anything. They only have a six pack."

"Yeah, yeah. Let's hope they don't ask," answered Billy. "I'm pooped. Time to hit the sack."

They all got up and headed up stairs. Suzy closed out her bad night by putting the beer bottle on the porch floor.

Emily and Caitlin were sleeping in a room with twin beds. Caitlin pulled the cotton blanket up to her chin with a big sigh of contentment.

"What's that all about?" asked Emily.

"A bad day for Suzy is a good one for me. Just keep Billy involved with basketball and I'll be happy."

"Caitlin, come on. We wouldn't be here at the beach if Suzy hadn't invited us.

"I know, but let me have my moment of triumph."

Emily woke up before Caitlin. She lay there for a while listening. The house was quiet. She decided to get up and see if there were the makings for pancakes in the kitchen. She rose quietly, slipped into a tee shirt and her jeans, and tiptoed downstairs.

She found a big box of mix in the pantry; the kind where all you needed to do was add water. There was a big pan in a bottom cabinet, some butter and syrup in the fridge and she was good to go. She had made a tall stack by the time Billy and Ralph made it downstairs. They were still debating which of them would sleep in the top bunk tonight. Billy had bullied the smaller Ralph into climbing up there last night. The boys made short work of the stack and Emily just kept cooking to get some for herself. Caitlin showed up, and the group, except for Dorothy and Suzy, began to fill their stomachs with pancakes. Ralph managed to get the coffee maker going to wash all those carbos down.

Dorothy arrived just about then. She said, "I'm going into the boys' bathroom. Suzy seems to be monopolizing ours. Why are you staring at me? My parents know that I have a beer occasionally. I even had a couple at my graduation party. Hell, I'm going to college 500 miles from here. They can't control me there. Relax. There won't be any problems. Save me some pancakes."

The Highlands called shortly after Dorothy returned and started eating pancakes. She announced that they would arrive by one in the afternoon and would bring subs for lunch.

Just then Suzy came down, her brow furrowed.

Ralph noticed a spot on her white shorts and what looked like blood dripping down her leg. "Hey", he said, "It looks like you're bleeding."

Dorothy snapped to attention. "Let's go up and look at that. Mom will kill me if you're hurt."

Suzy replied, "I must have scratched myself in the shower last night and knocked the scab off when I got dressed. It's nothing."

"Bleeding is never nothing," said Dorothy. She grabbed Suzy's arm and led her upstairs.

Emily heard some loud voices from up stairs and drifted to the foot of the stairs out of curiosity. All she could hear was Dorothy shouting.

"Why the hell did you do that, Suzy? Are you nuts? Let me see the rest of you."

"So, you made a fool of yourself last night, so what? We all do that sometimes. How do you think I felt when Dad insisted on driving those boys home from my graduation party? You need help. I'm gonna' tell Mom"

Then Emily heard Suzy scream, "You can't tell Mom. She'll freak!"

Dorothy screamed back, "You can't go on cutting yourself. I'm gonna be five hundred miles away. Who's gonna' help you?"

"I don't know. I don't know!"

There was complete silence for a moment. Emily felt terribly guilty and moved away from the stairs.

Fifteen minutes later the Highland girls came down, Dorothy in her bathing suit, Suzy in clean shorts and a tee shirt, her face freshly scrubbed.

Dorothy said, "Suzy's scratch is worse than it first looked. No ocean for her today."

"You'll be the queen of the beach," said Emily.

"Billy said, "In a sense she really is the queen of the beach. We wouldn't be here without her." He bowed before her with a grin.

Emily was delighted to see Suzy's face light up.

The crowd, including Dorothy, marched off to the beach on another beautiful late summer day. They duplicated yesterday's antics, slavered themselves with sunscreen, and plopped themselves down on the blankets for a brief rest before lunch. Suzy sat in a folding chair and shouted advice to all.

Meanwhile, either by plan or serendipity, the Highlands arrived a half hour ahead of schedule. The first thing Mr. Highland saw was the almost full beer bottle on the side porch. He inspected it, went to the recycle bin and found it empty. He found only pizza boxes in the trash barrel. He thought, *either it wasn't much of a party, or they were sober enough to clean up well afterward.*

He cornered Billy when the kids sauntered back from the beach, took him around to the side porch, and showed him the bottle still standing there and smelling like an old bar room in the hot sun. "How did this get here? Were you guys drinking last night?"

Billy hesitated only a moment and then answered the way he remembered lawyers coaching defendants to on TV. "I have no idea how that beer bottle got there. We weren't doing any drinking." All of which was strictly true.

Mr. Highland picked up the bottle, inspected its contents and said, "Nobody drank much out of this bottle anyway. Did Dorothy have visitors?"

There was no way Billy could duck that one without a blatant lie. He said, "Three of her classmates stopped by. They were sitting on the porch when we got back from our walk on the boardwalk."

Mr. Highland grunted. "OK, Billy, thanks. Get in there and grab yourself a sandwich before the vultures devour them all."

Billy let out a big sigh and fled.

Whatever transpired between Mr. Highland and his daughter never saw the light of day. Everybody had a great day and a half, and they all suffered through the massive traffic on the ride home.

CHAPTER TWELVE

Freshmen had to show up on Tuesday, a day before upper class students at EMR high school. At this point Emily's hair was long enough to band into a short ponytail and the 20 pounds she had added over the summer made her feel a little more grown up. In addition to the beginning bloom of her breasts, there was a little more "beef on her butt" as her mother called it. She wore some eye shadow and forgot all about the mole.

The program for the first day included greetings and other meetings, and a run-through of the full schedule of classes, though they were only half length. The confusion and the number of lost souls slowly died down as the day progressed.

On the bus home Suzy was in rare form. "I didn't get lost even once."

"Who are you trying to kid?" scoffed Bobby Martin. "You were standing in the middle of nowhere, and if I hadn't come by to give you directions, you'd still be there."

"Maybe, but girls are smart enough to ask for directions. You boys just wander around lost until somebody takes you by the hand and leads you to the right place."

Billy Pedrazi asked, "Emily, how did you make out after we left Algebra?"

Emily laughed. "I must confess I got lost once, but I was close. At the next building. Not too bad."

Billy said, "I was impressed with what was said at the big athletic meeting. Coach Cardello, the athletic director, looked like he would put up with no nonsense, and the head basketball coach gave a great speech."

"Yeah, Coach Walsh of the girls' team was very welcoming as well. He made a big point of saying that he was going to have the best dozen players in the school on his team. I was happy to hear the door was open to everybody. I can hope for next year if I do well on the freshman team."

Caitlin said, "I'll be happy on the freshman team and playing a lot, except they don't have a coach yet. The young man who was supposed to coach the team is in the hospital with cancer. The teams are going to wear tee shirts with his name on them as a sign of support for his remission."

"Yeah, that's terrible about him," Emily replied. "I like the tee shirt idea."

Suzy said, "More talk about basketball. You should see my LA teacher. He's a dream."

Emily said, "Do too much dreaming and you'll get an F." Everybody laughed, even Suzy.

The first home football game was the next Saturday. The hype started the first day of school at the welcoming assembly for all students. The head coach and the captains all gave speeches, the band played, the chorus sang, and everybody cheered. That done, both students and teachers got down to the serious business of learning. Homework was abundant.

Worse than the homework was the early time Emily had to get up to make the morning bus. School started 45 minutes earlier than it had at middle school, and the bus ride was long. She had to leave her house at 7:15 to catch the bus. Sometimes she didn't get any real breakfast even though her mother was up early to feed her father. Often, she was still a little groggy at the start of her first class: Algebra II.

Emily couldn't seem to get to sleep before eleven, even if she doggedly shut off her phone when she finished homework. She found that Caitlin was having the same problem. The shift in class time was hard to get used to. Janet was running herself ragged trying to blast Emily out of bed at 6:30, and there was little conversation on the bus ride. Emily almost welcomed rainy days when the cool water splashed on her face as she climbed out of the bus.

The football games were fun. About forty freshmen gathered in an upper corner of the bleachers at home games, wearing the black and gold school colors. They made up their own cheers. They tried to out shout the cheers from across the field, and they moaned when things went bad. They paid little attention to the well-orchestrated cheering squad in their black and gold sweaters, doing routines which did not seem to be related to the game. They cheered the performance of the band at half time and seemed to have more fun than the upper-class students. This went on even during the frigid night games toward the end of the season.

Of course, that was not the only way Emily spent her free time during the fall. There were "open gyms" to attend for those who aspired to play on the school's basketball teams in the winter. Football is king in New Jersey. Official basketball practice cannot start until the Monday before Thanksgiving, when all but a handful of football games are over. This spawns the "open gym" concept. Players show up during designated times to shoot around and maybe play some pick-up games to keep their eagerness in check. No coaches are allowed there to give instruction, but that doesn't preclude them from peeking around the corner to see who took the trouble to show up, and to see that players from last year were working on the skills they had been told needed improvement.

Emily, Caitlin, two girls from E. Hanover whom they had played against in eighth grade, Nicky Pelosi, and Josephine Alloco, gathered at one end of the court with a giant newcomer to the area named Sandy. Those from last year's teams congregated at the other. They seemed to consider themselves above fraternizing with the newcomers.

Sandy had moved to New Jersey from Chicago, Illinois when her father's job got transferred to New York. She was six feet two inches tall and had to weigh at least 180. Even though Emily had gained twenty pounds with her summer exercise and diet program, she was careful not to accidentally run into Sandy as they chased balls around the court. Sandy was slow moving and a little clumsy. Emily thought that perhaps she had just recently grown and was struggling to control her body. On top of that she had bad hands. The not so big E concluded she was definitely a project for whoever would coach the freshman team, though perhaps a standout a few years down the road. Sandy kept mostly to herself and would shoot at a side basket if the rest of the group wanted to play two on two. After several of these sessions Emily and Caitlin felt comfortable as they looked forward to the start of the season.

Another thing that happened to Emily, perhaps because of early morning grogginess, was trouble with Algebra II. On the other hand, she was the star of her first class after lunch: choir. Her teacher there offered her some private coaching to get her to sing more from her diaphragm and add power to her voice. She even hinted that there might be a spot for Emily in the school chorus and maybe even in the musical production planned for the spring.

Emily sought help from her father with the word problems with two unknowns which she found baffling. He tried to help, but the textbook baffled him also. "That's not the way I learned to solve these things," he moaned after another failed attempt to help his daughter make sense of her homework.

So, Emily asked Billy Pedrazi if he could help her. Though they had all exchanged cell phone numbers years ago, she had never called him. It felt funny, but she needed help, badly.

"Yeah, sure," he answered. "I get this stuff." He came over the next night after his open gym, and it was almost 10:30 before John drove him home.

Janet stuck her head into the bathroom while Emily was brushing her teeth. "That was a lot of work. Is the light beginning to dawn?"

"Absolutely. All I have to do is ignore the book and think logically. It's a little like the bathing suit problem. Get rid of the unnecessary data, define what you know and what you're trying to find out, and create a relationship to give you the answer."

"I'm not sure I follow the whole analogy, but if you see the light, that's all I ask."

"I'm good, Mom. Billy was awesome at explaining how to work those problems."

"Good. Get to bed so you don't forget how to do it. When's the next test?"

"Two days from now. Plenty of time to work some extra problems and ace it."

Janet smiled and went downstairs to wait for her husband to return. She was happy to note that her daughter's competitive nature extended to things other than basketball.

Both Caitlin and Suzy were clamoring to get Billy to help them with their Algebra problems at lunch the next day after listening to Emily's new confidence. They may have decided that there was more than one way to get on the good side of a handsome young classmate.

CHAPTER THIRTEEN

The first day of freshman basketball practice at East Morris Regional High School was a disaster for Emily. She simply could not go. She had to spend almost three hours in the orthodontist's chair undergoing the inevitable rite of passage to which most suburban girls are subjected. It had taken two months lead time to set the date for the ordeal, and the conflict with the first day of practice had not been recognized at the time. Life could not have been worse for Emily.

Her mouth was sore the next day, for which she was taking Tylenol every four hours. She was also having a little trouble speaking clearly around the hardware in her mouth, but she was not about to miss practice two days in a row. She had been told that the new coach was a hard taskmaster.

There had to be a new coach because the forty-year-old father of three who had coached the team for the last five years had come down with cancer. EMR high school athletic director, Phil Cardello, introduced Mrs. Sarah Murdock to the team on the first day of practice and announced that the school had been blessed to have lured her out of retirement to coach the team at the last minute. Mrs. Murdock had coached varsity teams in Hudson County for a decade before retiring.

EMR had a "no-cut" policy for freshman sports so that there were fifteen girls besides Emily bouncing balls in the small auxiliary gym when coach arrived for practice. Emily introduced herself to a frowning Mrs. Murdock.

"Where were you yesterday?" she asked.

Emily pointed to her mouth. "Getting these."

91

"And you could not have scheduled that appointment so that it didn't conflict with the first day of practice? Isn't basketball important to you?"

Emily was flummoxed. "It took months to set the date. I had to have two teeth pulled; there was a lot of stuff. I'm sorry to have missed the first day."

"Well, you had better work hard to catch up."

Emily put the dual level mouthpiece with the breathing hole between levels into her mouth and soon found out what that meant. Practice was made up of 90 minutes of drills: dribbling drills, layup drills, passing drills, boxing out drills, and then suicide sprints followed by foul shooting practice. There was no scrimmage, no play. Caitlin had told Emily that coach had lectured yesterday that she was proud of the fact that her teams always had better skills than their opponents, and that there was no better place to start that than at the freshman level. In addition, she spent a lot of time with Sandy, trying to bring her to the point where her size could be an advantage.

Emily felt that she could use a lot of practice with her left hand, so worked on doing things with her left hand during the drills. She was correct in that but didn't realize that she was creating a not-so-skilled first impression on her new coach.

There were about three weeks of practice scheduled before the opening game on a Friday in mid-December. The drills continued day after day at practice. The varsity and JV had three scrimmages against other schools, but coach Murdock declined to do that, claiming her team was not ready. She was right in that. She did not introduce any offensive system until the Monday of the week of the first game. Walk-throughs were disjointed with girls running to designated spots on the floor like robots regardless of what was happening with the ball. Emily rarely got on the court for those.

Coach Murdock consented to an informal scrimmage against the JV on the Tuesday before the opener on Friday. That was not good for the confidence of the freshman team. Their big girl, Sandy, was left in the dust, and had no idea what to do. Caitlin and the two players from East Hanover did their best to run the offense but were no match for the JV. Emily never got off the bench.

A full ration of suicides and foul shots was ordered after the scrimmage, while Coach Murdock worked with Sandy on positioning and foot work. At the end of practice, she brought her clipboard to the foul shooters to record how many shots they each had made from ten attempts. Five or six was the norm. Almost as an afterthought she asked Emily for her count.

"Ten," answered Emily with a shrug.

"This is not a joke," said Coach Murdock with a frown.

"Neither is missing foul shots. I made all ten."

The coach stared at Emily for a moment and then wrote "10?" on her sheet.

The freshman team got to play in the big gym on Friday afternoon for the first time. Their game was at four, to be followed by the JV at about 5:30 and then the varsity at seven. They were playing Roxbury, a school about twenty miles west of EMR, who showed up with only eight girls. Several had missed the bus, which left on schedule. Delaying the start of a triple header was not acceptable.

As the horn blew to signal the end of warm-ups two girls from Roxbury came running into the gym dressed in their uniforms. They had apparently scrounged a ride to the game. The Roxbury coach welcomed them with open arms and added their names to the official score book, shiny new for the new season.

The referees, an older man and a young woman who looked as if she had just graduated from high school, noticed the change, and conferred. The younger official insisted that they call the technical foul for adding the names to the book which the rules required. The Roxbury coach just raised his arms in surrender.

Coach Murdock looked down the bench and said, "Barker, you claim to be an expert foul shooter. Get in there and shoot the technicals. Let's see if you can make a foul shot when it counts."

Emily pulled off her warm-up shirt thinking, *she didn't believe I made 10 of 10 at practice the other day*. Adrenaline blasted into her veins. She took a deep breath and said, "Sure Coach."

She replaced Sandy in the starting lineup and walked to the foul line at the opposite end of the floor from her bench. The young official bounced the ball to her as she stood alone at the foul line. Something was wrong. The ball bounced too high and felt like a rock. Emily bounced the ball from head high to check, and then turned to the older official. She said, "There's way too much air in this ball."

The official took the ball and tested the bounce himself. He laughed. "You're very right, young lady. That happens a lot in the first week of a season. The equipment managers just fill the balls according to the pressure stamped on them and never test the bounce." He reached into his pocket and removed an inflation pin. He let some air out, tested the ball again, let more air out, and then found the bounce to his liking. He flipped the ball to the woman official, who was a little red in the face, and said, "Let's start again."

The woman bounced the ball to Emily, who went through her usually pre-shot routine, and fired away. The ball hit the front rim, then the back and finally fell through the basket. Emily shook her head. *Come on, Bro. You can do this in your sleep,* she thought. She prepared again and this time the ball fell through the basket with only the swish of nylon.

Caitlin gave her a big high five and Coach Murdock promptly replaced her in the lineup. Emily never got off the bench again during the game, which they lost in a sea of turnovers. In the post game meeting Coach Murdock said only, "We have practice in this gym at ten tomorrow morning. Don't be late."

■ ■ ■ ■ ■ ■ ■

Natasha Booker came to scout Morris Brown's new conference opponent, EMR, that evening. As usual she was dressed in designer jeans and heels, not the four inch high ones she had broken in Pittsburgh though. As her wont, she came early to see some of the JV game and meet the EMR coach and AD. At half time of the JV game, she caught up with Doug Walsh, the varsity coach and introduced herself.

"Welcome to the conference, "Doug said with a smile. "I hear you guys are pretty good. Maybe we'll develop into a neighborhood rivalry."

"I hear you're pretty good too. I've come to see for myself. We don't open until tomorrow."

"We're pretty young. We'll have to see how it goes."

Natasha laughed. "Very coachly, Doug. I didn't see Emily Barker on the JV squad. Is she some of that youth you were talking about on the varsity?"

"Emily Barker? No, she may be on the freshman team. Why do you ask?"

Coach Booker was not about to give any tips to an opposing coach. "Oh, I saw her in the eighth-grade championship game and thought she had potential."

"Yeah, I never got to see any of the middle school playoff games because of baseball. I haven't seen any of the freshman practice either. It's been hectic."

"Well, Doug good luck tonight. I'll be taking notes."

Doug said, "I look forward to playing you guys. It's in about three weeks I think."

"Just about. See you." She climbed up to the top row of the bleachers in her high heels with the ease of someone who had done that many times.

EMR eked out a win against Roxbury and looked young in the process.

Doug showed up at the gym just before ten the next morning. He caught up with Coach Murdock. "Tough loss yesterday," he said.

She replied, "We'll get better when I get our big up to speed."

"How did Emily Barker do?"

"Why do you ask?"

"She was on the county eighth grade championship team. I heard she had potential."

"She's a tween-er. Not big enough to play the post and not quick enough to be a good guard. Just a fill-in. She may be a good foul shooter, though."

"Her experience might help with the turnovers."

That comment pushed the wrong button. "Coach Walsh, when I took this job, I was assured that I could handle my team my way; that nobody would tell me who to play or what tactics to use."

Doug backed up a whole stride. "Whoa, coach. I'm not telling you what to do. It was just a thought."

"Think what you want. You're still inexperienced by my standards. This is my team and I've been promised I can run it my way."

Doug said, "Yes Ma'am." And went to a corner of the gym where he sat on a chair to watch the practice. It was the first time he had seen any of the freshman players. Practice started with a walk through of the offense. That was followed by the usual drills and ended with the suicides and foul shots.

He noticed that Emily did most of the ball drills left-handed but shot her foul shots right-handed. She was pretty good left-handed and made all ten of her foul shots with the other hand.

Emily and Caitlin stayed after practice for a few minutes to work on their moves and shooting. Doug was impressed with Emily's foot work and the timing she and Caitlin showed. They could both shoot well, Caitlin from the arc and Emily from the foul line in. On top of that, Emily could jump high enough to touch the rim. He had girls on the varsity taller than Emily who couldn't do that.

Before practice on Monday Phil Cardello called Doug into his office. "Coach Murdock tells me you've been complaining how she's running the freshman team."

"What! Phil, I asked about one of her players, mentioned by an opposing coach who thought she might be on my varsity squad. The girl played on the eighth-grade county championship team last year. She never got in the freshman game Friday."

"Doug, you know we had a hell of a time finding someone to coach that team at the last minute. I had to plead with Mrs. Murdock to take the job. I made all sorts of promises. You can't screw all that up. She'll quit."

"Phil, I'm in this for the long haul. I have a big interest in who's in the pipeline. Can we let some rent-a-coach screw that up? I watched this kid, Barker, stay after practice to work on her moves and shooting. She can get up and touch the rim!"

Phil spoke in a quieter tone. "Easy, Doug. Let's not let our ethnic tempers screw this conversation up. You can't go and tell Mrs. Murdock who to play. What would you do if you were in her shoes and that happened?"

Doug spoke more quietly too. "I don't know what I'd do in that case, Phil, but I'm going to do some research on the Barker kid. I'll start with calling her eighth-grade coach and follow the thread. I'll be back here in a day or so."

"OK, but be creative."

Doug caught up with Coach Costello on the phone at Ridge School the next day. He got the whole story, including the 16U summer team and the fact that Natasha Booker had been the coach of that team.

He sat with Phil Cardello again before practice. "Phil, we agreed long ago that I get first dibs on talent for my varsity squad, right?"

"Yessss, but. . ."

"But nothing. I want to move Barker up. She played on an AAU 16 U team out of Morristown last summer that won the championship of a tournament in Pittsburgh that had 32 teams in it. It's insane that she's sitting on the end of the freshman bench."

"How the hell are we going to do that, Doug?"

"Phil, you've got all those advanced degrees and certifications. Figuring out how to do it without losing Coach Murdock is why they pay you so much more than me."

Phil had to laugh. Then he was quiet for a long moment. "What if the girl doesn't want to do that?"

"What kid who played over her head all summer wouldn't want to take the shot?"

"That's probably right. What if she strikes out?"

"The worst that can happen is that she'll land on the JV bench. At the very least she'll be practicing with us every day and not get lost."

There was another long period of silence. Finally, Phil said, "I'll talk to the kid when the team gets back from the game at West Morris this evening. I'm going to verify the story you got and see what her attitude is. I'll get back to you tomorrow. By the way good luck out there yourself. They're usually pretty good."

"Yeah, but I think we can handle them. We play Dover here on Friday. They're pretty weak. We ought to be able to get Barker some minutes somewhere then."

"Don't make any plans until you hear from me."

Phil Cardello intercepted Emily when the freshman bus returned after the game that evening. He had no idea how to begin the conversation, so started with the obvious. "How did you guys make out?"

Emily wore a big frown. She said, "We lost again. Can't seem to get many points, and they were pretty good."

"As good as the 16 U team you played on this summer?"

Emily blurted, "Well no. How do you know about that?"

"As I was told earlier today: that's why they pay me so much. Did you play much today?"

"No. Just the last minute of garbage time."

"How do you feel about that?"

Emily didn't know how to answer that. Tell the truth? Or would that just bury her in Coach Murdock's doghouse? Why was the AD asking her this question? "Mr. Cardello, there's no way I know how to answer that. I've never had this kind of question from a coach in my life."

"I'm trying to solve a potential problem, Emily. Will you help me?"

Emily remembered Billy's comment about the impression he had of Mr. Cardello' speech on the first day of class. Her pent-up frustration won the day. She blurted, "I don't think I'm a head case, but I know I can help this team be better. I started off in coach Murdock's doghouse 'cause I missed the first day of practice to get these."

She gestured toward her mouth full of hardware, and went on, "I don't think Coach Murdock believed that I made all 10 of my fouls shots at practice one day before our opening game. I suspect she tried to show me up by putting me in to shoot the two technicals at the start of that game. I made both shots, and maybe that embarrassed her. I sat on the bench for the rest of the game."

"You sound like you're ready to quit."

"I've never quit on anything in my life. I'll keep working."

"I really appreciate your being honest. Do you know some of the girls on the JV?"

"Yes. I played with two of them and against a couple more two years ago. I was smaller then."

"And do you think you could play with them now?"

"Yeah. I watched the games Friday night."

"Do you know Coach Booker from Morris Brown?"

"Sure. She coached the 16U team I played on."

"Do you think she would recommend you for our JV team?"

Emily was flummoxed. She sputtered, "You'd have to ask her that."

Mr. Cardello paused a long moment, looked up at the ceiling as if seeking divine guidance, and finally locked eyes with Emily.

"Would you like a chance to play on the JV?"

Emily stiffened. She thought, *how could anything like that be possible?* She felt the Adrenalin rush, her face flush. She said, "Give me a fair chance, and I'll live with the results."

The AD continued to look into Emily's eyes for another moment, then said, "Report to Coach Walsh in the big gym for practice tomorrow. I'll take care of telling everybody. And good luck."

Emily was struck dumb. She saw her mother come into the gym to pick her up. She waved at her and held up one finger. Her heart was racing as she went into the locker room to get the books she would need for homework. *What should she tell her mother? When? If her father ever found out at how she was being treated on the freshman team, he would go into orbit. He'll get to a game soon and the cat will be out of the bag. What if she stinks up the place on the JV and ends up back on the freshman bench, with the coach saying I told you so?* She stopped her thoughts there. She'd never stunk up the game at any level. She would say nothing to nobody until the results were in.

Her mother rarely asked a lot of questions about her games, so it was easy to shrug off the few she did ask on the trip home. Emily was fidgety at dinner and escaped as soon as she could to do her homework. She also turned off her cell phone. Eventually she slept.

She awoke without any nagging the following morning and arrived in the kitchen in time to eat a good breakfast. Her mother was puzzled but asked no questions. She would find out soon enough.

Emily walked hesitantly into the big gym that afternoon. The girls' team practiced from 2:45 until 4:15, when the boys took over. The schedule alternated every other week so that the benefits of getting home early and being able to practice longer were shared equally.

Coach Walsh came to greet her almost immediately. About half of the combined JV and varsity squads of 22 girls was there ahead of her, just shooting around and tying their shoes. Walsh took her to meet Coach Simmons, the JV coach, who also assisted with the varsity team. Coach Walsh blew his whistle precisely at 2:45 and gathered the girls at the bench. He took Emily by the arm and drew her in front of the group.

"Girls, this is Emily Barker. Some of you played with or against her a couple of years ago. I've invited her to spend a few days with us to see how it goes. I expect you all to give her a hand when it's needed."

He gave them all a minute to digest the surprise and then said, "OK two lines. Let's get loose."

There were drills at the varsity practice too. They consumed less of the time and Emily did them right-handed when appropriate. Then the varsity scrimmaged for a quarter on the full court, interrupted often by Coach Walsh to refine either the offense or defense. While that was going on, Coach Simmons took a few minutes away from commenting on the scrimmage to point out to Emily what both the O and the D were trying to do.

Then the JV took its turn to scrimmage. After four minutes of the game, Emily was inserted along with the other sub.

She had no trouble with the man-to-man defense, but was a little lost on offense, aside from the fast breaks. Rebounding is the same at any level though, and she went to the boards like a tiger. At the defensive end she whipped the outlet pass to a guard and sprinted down the court just as she had in the summer. As at the start of the summer there was no return pass, but her effort put her in position to rebound at the offensive end. She got a couple and put one back for a basket. Coach Walsh missed none of this as he pointed out the misplays of the JV to his varsity team.

This practice also ended with foul shot practice. They used the four side baskets as well as the main ones in groups for four, mostly segregated by which squad the girls were on. There was lots of chatter during this exercise and some razzing about each miss. No comments were directed at Emily though, even when she missed the last of ten she tried. She noted Mr. Cardello watching from the corner of the gym and wondered how long he had been there.

Coach Walsh put a hand on Emily's arm as they filed out of the gym and said, "See you tomorrow."

Her heart gave that little leap it always did when she got over a hurdle. Not that tomorrow wouldn't present another one, but as her father liked to say: "the only way to eat an elephant is one bite at a time." There would be no stopping the onslaught of questions from Caitlin now. Emily had to prepare some noncommittal answers.

The last text from Caitlin that night said, "We'll miss you. Tear them a new one."

Thursday's practice was a lot like Wednesday's except that there was a chalk talk about how to deal with Dover's zone defense. Once again, the key element was to play through the high post to move the ball from side to side for open shots.

They scrimmaged half court at both ends today, the JV at one end, the varsity at the other. The defense played Dover's zone and the offense the high post system. It was soon clear to Emily that this was the same system she had played in last season and during the summer. When her chance to play offense came, she demonstrated her familiarity very effectively. She made herself available in good timing so the guards could pass her the ball, passed it quickly to one side or the other or underneath. She even turned to face the basket one time when she felt no pressure and sank a shot herself. It could not have gone better.

Coach Simmons said, "See the trainer tomorrow and get a proper JV jersey. Just keep the freshman shirt for now. We'll gather in the aux gym just after half time of the freshman game for a walk through."

Emily just said, "Yes sir."

———————

The Dover freshman team was weak. EMR won by ten. They were happy to get a win. Caitlin was the high scorer with 12. Even Sandy got four points.

The JV game was no different. The EMR subs got into the game early and were soon into the flow. The team warmed up to Emily at the high post and appreciated her efforts on defense. The number of fans assembled was small until half time, but her father had found his usual seat in the first row near the division line. Her mother sat just behind him. The varsity spectators began to file in around half time. Some of them got a kick out of Emily blocking a couple of Dover's shots. When the game was over, several of the JVs, including Emily, were asked to sit on the bench for the varsity game. Emily could feel her father bursting with optimism.

The Dover varsity was little better than their JV. EMR was ahead by 15 at half time and grew the lead as the third quarter progressed, despite playing the substitutes the whole time. Coach Walsh began working the JV players into the game at the start of the fourth quarter.

Emily got in with five minutes left. She had been bouncing up and down on her chair since half time. Her heart was racing. She was so fired up she couldn't stand still while waiting for the ball to come alive after her substitution. Dover had a throw-in. Emily was guarding a girl an inch or so shorter. When a pass came toward that girl, Emily leaped into its path, stole the ball, and streaked toward the basket. No one could get anywhere near her, and she made the layup. The fire did not go out. Emily had three rebounds, a blocked shot and had two more baskets in the next three minutes, when her time came to an end.

Coach Walsh said, "Emily, I'm sorry, but I gotta take you out. You're rubbing salt in their wounds, and we can't do that. I can't ask you not to play hard. There will be another game."

Emily looked at the score board and saw that EMR was now ahead by 25. She said, "Sorry, Coach. I didn't think. I was excited."

"If I were you, I would have done the same. Relax. We have practice tomorrow. It won't be so easy from now on."

Caitlin ran up to Emily after the game and gave her a big hug. "Wait until Coach Murdock hears about this. I bet her face will be red."

"Don't you tell her. You could take my place in her doghouse."

Caitlin just laughed, saw Emily's father coming and escaped.

He said, "You didn't tell me you were on the varsity squad."

"I'm not. This was a special event because Dover is so weak. Hopefully I'll be on the JV bench for the next game."

"Hopefully? That doesn't sound like you."

"Dad, I got a special break to even get a chance at that. I need to keep performing to hold my spot."

Her father was dumbfounded. He was missing something. He had many more questions, but Emily was saved by the arrival of her mother. They hugged, her sweat notwithstanding.

"I'll be out in a minute. I need to change." Nobody showered after a game anymore.

CHAPTER FOURTEEN

And so the season went on. When the boys' teams played at home, the girls played away, and vice versa. As a result, Emily never got to watch Billy play. Sometimes the boys' freshman team went on a separate bus from the JV and varsity, so Billy got back in time to see Emily play a bit toward the end of her JV game. They would compare notes about their games on the bus and in the moments before and after their Algebra class. Billy was starting on his freshman team and playing well. So far, the stars of the Ridge School eighth grade teams were living up to their own hopes and expectations.

Suzy went to all the games she could and led the cheering. She was especially vocal on the school bus the morning after games. According to her, Billy's JV coach watched his every move and was about to promote him. She had the statistics to show he was the leading scorer on the freshman team. Billy looked embarrassed at all this praise but kept his mouth shut. With what she overheard at the beach house Emily felt apprehensive about Suzy's behavior, but she too kept her mouth shut.

Both varsity teams were participating in Christmas tournaments at nearby Chatham, but there were none for the JV or freshman teams. They just got to practice every day during the Christmas break and go to support the varsity at their games. Emily, Caitlin, Billy, and Suzy were back together again cheering for both teams. EMR won the girls championship, but the boys lost in the semifinals to New Providence.

Grades for the first semester came soon after. Emily worked hard at Algebra and spent an hour on the phone with Billy Pedrazi reviewing what he taught her about solving word problems. She got B+ for the semester. She also did at least that well in all her other courses, including an A+ in

Choir. She didn't know how well she would have done if she had gone to Queens College Prep but felt satisfied with her first steps toward an academic record worthy of acceptance to an elite college.

As she got more familiar with the system and her JV teammates, Emily got more playing time, and eventually worked her way into the starting lineup. There were two girls slightly taller than she on the JV, but none could match her jumping ability. She was not playing in the low post often though. Her coaches wanted her to get familiar with all the roles on the court. They even worked with her on three-point shots.

This progress had not quite reached fruition when the first game at Morris Brown came up. It was at MB. Coach Booker greeted Emily when she came on the floor to warm up for the JV game. "Hello, Bones. You don't look as much like the praying mantis you did this summer. You've grown yourself a ponytail and put on what ---- twenty pounds? I guess we'll have to find a new nickname for you. Have you been lifting?"

"Hi, Coach B. Yeah, I got tired of being pushed around so much. I need to thank you."

"For What?

"Apparently your question about me to Coach Walsh prompted what led to my being promoted from the end of the freshman bench. I appreciate that."

"That wasn't too smart of me. Now I'm faced with more competition."

"We'll see how much it will hurt," said Emily with a smile.

Coach B said, "Have a good one" and slapped Emily on the butt.

Emily got into the game near the end of the first quarter. That reminded her of her early days with the AAU team. She went to work with the same enthusiasm she did during the summer. Though she was still building her credibility with her new teammates, she used her rebounding skill to make an impact in the second quarter. She scored 4 points and had three assists from the high post.

As she came off the court at half time Jo and Ty came to give her a hug and say, "good luck". They were seniors this year and already had their game faces on for the varsity game. They all laughed at the situation where ex teammates who had been through some wars together were now competitors.

The second half was close. The girls from MB were boxing out better under the boards and getting some easy baskets. Emily got into the game early in the third quarter and played the rest of the way. She battled the bigger MB girls fiercely for rebounds at both ends, blocked a couple of shots, but still got pushed around some. She actually got a return pass as she sprinted down the lane on a fast break she started with a defensive rebound. She made the layup and was fouled. She made the foul shot to bring her point total to nine, but that was not enough to win the game. EMR lost 45-40.

Amid mutterings about the unfairness of having to play teams that were able to recruit players, the JV team donned their sweats, and climbed into the bleachers to watch the varsity game. Emily's father followed them to sit next to her and whisper congratulations on a fine game.

She whispered her reply, "Dad, now isn't the time. We lost the game."

"Yeah, but you were great."

"It's not all about me, Dad. Look I think Mom's waving to you."

John looked up at the ceiling. "OK, I get the message. I'll leave. It will be interesting to see how Ty and Jo do in this game."

"Yeah, it will."

Emily settled in at the edge of the group of teammates to cheer the varsity on and maybe learn something. She found herself of two minds: Rooting for her team to win but wanting to see Jo and Ty play well. She had been through several wars with Ty and Jo, shared a lot of sweat, tears and success with them. She had none of that experience with the varsity girls, most of whom she hardly knew at this point. And while she was getting closer to her JV teammates, it still wasn't yet the same level of intensity she had developed with her AAU comrades. She limited herself to discussions of strategic issues and observations about skillful plays as the game went on.

EMR lost 60-52. Ty and Jo were both outstanding. Several of the other players also were talented. MB was going to be tough for years to come. Emily was still surprised that the MB head coach didn't have a heart attack.

The short bus ride back to school was filled with more complaints about playing against teams that could recruit players. Coach Walsh told them to stop whining, but all that did was reduce the complaints to whispers.

"Did you see that big black girl rebound? We had nobody that big. Where the hell did they get her?"

Emily wanted to say, "Newark" and "She isn't the biggest girl we might play against," but kept her mouth shut. Hadn't any of the varsity girls played somewhere in the summer?

Her father picked her up at the gym, and lavished praise on her about her play all the way home.

The team had the weekend off. Emily found herself in the starting lineup for the JV at Monday's practice. The girl's team had the late practice that day, so the freshman team was done by the time the varsity and JV practice started. Coach Murdock watched for perhaps ten minutes, shook her head, and left. Emily couldn't guess what she was thinking. The freshman team had won only one game so far, and Caitlin had told her that Sandy hadn't made much progress.

As the season wore on, Emily became a bigger force on the JV team. She played with great energy and began scoring more points, but did not try to be a superhero. There were sophomores and one junior to compete for that role. The team was winning and gearing up for the home game against Morris Brown, the only team that had beaten either the varsity or JV.

That last game of the season was on a Tuesday night at home. EMR had to win to tie for the conference championship. The stands were packed by the time the JV game started in anticipation of the crucial varsity contest. The JV had never played before such a large and enthusiastic crowd. Somehow John scrounged his usual seat in the first row at midcourt.

Coach Booker had nothing to say to Emily before this game. She was all business.

Emily gathered the starters during the moment that the JV team waited on the court before the opening tip. "Look, we can beat these guys. Let's crank it up a notch and use our heads." They put their hands together and shouted, "Yeah, let's get them."

The game was a doozey. It started out slowly, like two heavyweight boxers feeling each other out. Then the pace picked up, shots began to fall, and Adrenaline charged everybody's blood stream. Every rebound, every shot was contested; bodies hit the floor chasing loose balls, and tempers sometimes flared. The referees had their hands full.

With 30 seconds left MB was ahead 41-40, but EMR had foul shots: a one plus one penalty. Emily was lined up in the second lane space next to a girl a couple of inches taller. She called encouragement to her teammate and then tensed to go after the rebound if there was one.

Unfortunately for EMR there was one, and the girl next to Emily leaped into the lane to box her out. Emily spun around the girl's back to get in front of her as she came down with the ball. Emily drove her hand up under the ball in the girl's arms and popped it three feet straight up.

She then bounced off the floor to snatch the ball away from her opponent. She was immediately surrounded by both MB rebounders, making a put back shot impossible.

Emily pivoted away from the pressure and passed the ball to teammate Nicky outside the arc. She started to follow that pass away from the basket, but then cut back into the foul shooter's semicircle. There she caught a return pass and made a move. With her left foot as pivot, she stepped to the right drawing a counter move from the big girl forced into guarding her. Immediately she reversed directions, lifting her right foot and swinging it to the left past the defender's hip. A classic crossover move. She leaped toward the basket off that foot and started her shot left-handed. Just as it left her hand, she was sent sprawling by her defender. The whistle blew.

From the floor she looked toward the basket to see if her shot had been successful. She was horrified to see the referee standing in the lane shouting, "No basket," and signaling a traveling violation. Emily leaped to her feet and screamed, "I never moved my pivot foot!"

The man put his whistle near his mouth and shouted, "Knock it off, kid."

At the same moment Coach Simmons shouted, "Emily!"

Emily instantly realized that her team could ill afford a technical foul at that point, so swallowed whatever else she had been tempted to say.

Coach Simmons went on to instruct, "If we don't get a steal on the throw-in, foul."

Emily went to do jumping jacks in front of the thrower-in. They did not get the steal and fouled the girl who caught the pass. The girl calmly made two free throws. A last-second shot by EMR was no good and the game was over. Emily sank to her knees. Three teammates came to lift her up.

As the teams and coaches passed each other in the line shaking hands after the game, Coach Booker stopped Emily and gave her a gentle hug. She said, "That was a hell of a game, Emily. The guy blew the call. We have to live with those. I damn near screwed myself with my big mouth, but it was a pleasure to see you grow. See you this summer."

Emily just nodded. She still couldn't trust herself to speak.

Her parents caught up with her just after the post game meeting with Coach Simmons. They both hugged their sweaty daughter, who was still breathing hard. John's face was flushed. He said, "Emily I think that was the best game I've seen you play. You had 15 points and eight rebounds.

I'd be willing to bet that no freshman has ever done that well in a critical JV game."

"Whatever, Dad. We still lost."

"Yeah, but you really won it with that move we worked on in the back yard. The guy made a mistake."

"At least I didn't hear you shouting at him."

Janet said, "And he didn't do that. I think I could hear his teeth grinding even in all the noise, but your father kept his promise not to shout at referees anymore."

Emily had to smile. "I understand that temptation better now. I almost lost it out there. Maybe it's in the genes." They shared a group hug. "Did you save me a seat for the varsity game?"

The varsity game was not such a doozey. Ty was too big and strong for the shorter "big" girls on the EMR varsity to handle. MB kept getting the ball to Ty up high enough so that it could not be contested consistently, and Ty had the touch this night. Having played against Ty a lot during the summer Emily thought she might have had a couple of tricks up her sleeve to slow the big girl down, but she was not playing. She gave Ty and Jo a hug and wished them well in the tournaments to come. Basketball was over for Emily for the season.

Not so, it turned out. Coach Walsh took her aside at the Varsity practice the next day. "You have a choice, Emily. You can sit on the varsity bench Saturday in our state tournament game, or you can play with freshman team in the round robin event organized by the Breast Cancer Society to raise funds for research. It's not likely that there'll be a chance for you to get in the varsity game, but you never know, and you might learn something."

"Great," replied Emily. "I can get to know some of the varsity girls a little."

"You're pretty quick to blow off your classmates."

That stopped Emily cold. After a moment she said, "If I'm going to sit on a bench, it might as well be the varsity's"

"I have a promise from Coach Murdock that you will play every minute your legs will hold you up. The tournament will be structured like an AAU tournament. Each team will play at least two games, and the best two will play a third. There's a complicated system to determine who plays the final."

"Are you saying that Coach Murdock asked for me to play on her team?"

"Yes."

"Why didn't she ask me herself?"

"I have first dibs on your body," Walsh said with a smile. "She had to ask me first."

"She still could have asked me herself."

"Emily, put yourself in her shoes. Do you think it was easy for her to come to me and admit she was wrong about you? Are you into kicking people when they're down?"

Emily looked down at the floor. She'd love to kick that nasty old . . . lady somewhere. Even if she played a lot, fumble-fingered Sandy would still be the focus of the team. She might not even see the ball much. "I don't know, Coach. Playing for her would be hard. What do you think I should do?"

"It's your call, but I think you should consider two things: playing at least two more games is better than sitting, and what do you think Caitlin would advise?"

"You just laid a lot of pressure on me."

"You're not a baby anymore."

Out of the corner of her eye she saw a figure appear in the doorway that led to the auxiliary gym. It was Caitlin. She folded her hands in front of her chest as if in prayer. Emily had to laugh at that. Caitlin made a beckoning gesture. Emily threw her hands up in surrender.

Walsh said, "Give 'em hell Emily."

Coach Murdock said nothing to Emily and was all business as practice started. "We're going to have to change the scheme of things some now that Emily will be playing with us." She turned around a white marker board with several play diagrams on it. *She had clearly anticipated this situation,* realized Emily. *Was that a compliment to my class loyalty, or to Caitlin's persuasive charm? Oh well, I'm here now.*

They practiced for three days, and Emily found herself very much in the thick of things. There were plays for her at both the high and low posts, some of which she had never seen before. She and Caitlin worked after the team left at getting the timing and location of passes right. It felt good to play with her again.

The one-day charity tournament was being played at Morris Knolls High School where two games could be played simultaneously. Referees were being donated by the local referees' organization. They had chosen the best of the most recent class to pass through the testing program and sent a supervisor to observe the rookies' performance. Calling them rookies was misleading. The two men assigned to the EMR game were both fathers. They officiated other sports and were just adding to their brand. Their supervisor was their teacher and looked to be 75 or so. He was short, losing his hair, and sounded demanding, mean even, as he briefed his charges before the game.

EMR's first game was against West Morris. Unlike Coach Booker with her high heels and designer jeans, Coach Murdock was dressed very conservatively. She was wearing a black business suit, low heeled shoes, and a gold blouse. The school colors in a very subdued package.

During warm-ups Caitlin came to Emily and said, "Guess who's on that team."

"Who?" asked Emily.

"Number 14 is the fat kid who played for Frosythe in eighth grade basketball and pitched for them in softball."

Emily studied the opponents. "Oh yeah," she said. "It will be fun to get some revenge, even if it's a year after the fact."

And they got revenge. Emily and Caitlin were hot, and their antagonist just couldn't keep up. Emily left 14 standing on the wrong foot on several trips down the floor. When 14 got help in covering Emily, she was able to pass the ball to an open teammate and get to the boards for rebounds despite being held and pushed in ways the rookie referees either didn't see or didn't know what to do about. These days Emily did not fall often under such abuse. She just got even. With three minutes left in the game EMR was ahead by 15, and Coach Murdock sent five subs to the table to signal she thought the game was in hand.

Number 14 saw this and literally tackled Emily as she stretched up for a pass at the high post. Emily crashed to the floor with Number 14 falling on top of her. The combination knocked the wind out of her. She lay there stunned and gasping for air. Coach Murdock exploded off her bench screaming for 14 to be ejected and rushed to Emily's side to see how she was. The stunned referees blew their whistles urgently and went to their supervisor for advice.

Number14 jumped up and stood over Emily with a smirk on her face. The smirk lasted only a moment until Sandy arrived and punched her on the jaw, knocking her down. The site manager got there just a step behind Sandy. He put himself between 14 and Sandy, but there was no sign of fight in 14. He gently backed Sandy away from the area.

Emily sat up, surrounded by Caitlin and Coach Murdock, and still struggling for air. Her parents stood a few feet onto the court, uncertain about what to do. All the players from both teams stood in an amazed semicircle on the bench side of the court and the referees took positions to prevent any further interaction between the players. The lone policeman hired for security at this supposedly friendly tournament came from the other court to see what the excitement was. He stopped too. The tournament director came rushing into the gym from the concession area, a look of horror on her face. Everyone just stood there while Emily struggled to recover.

After what seemed an eternity, the tournament director and site manager moved into a far corner to caucus. Coach Murdock resumed her demand for 14 to be banned from the tournament. The West Morris coach, who was a foot taller than Coach Murdock, retaliated with caustic comments about just rewards for running up the score. The two stood shouting at each other, a Mutt and Jeff comic book pair for those old enough to remember. Soon everybody stopped talking and waited for the two in the corner to reveal the result of their discussion. The director pulled out her cell phone and pushed a button. It was clear that it would take a few more minutes for any decision to be reached.

Meanwhile, Caitlin helped Emily to her feet. Emily walked around a bit followed by Caitlin, and then went to her parents. "I'm OK," she said. "Just had the wind knocked out of me."

Her father said, "I remember that . . . girl. She was the one who got away with pushing you around in the Forsythe game a year ago."

"Yeah," said Emily. "But we put her in her place today."

"What's going to happen?" asked Janet.

"Who knows? This is friggin ridiculous," mused Emily.

"Ems, language!" snapped Janet.

"OK, Mom, OK"

At last, the management duo approached the scorer's table and took the microphone used to introduce the players at the start of the game. In a shaky voice the director said, "Players, coaches, and friends of basketball and breast cancer, this game is over. The score stands. Number 14 from West Morris and the big girl from East Morris, number 25 I think, are banned from further play in this tournament and their school administration will be notified of this deplorable behavior. If there is any further flagrant behavior from any team, the whole tournament will be canceled."

She shut off the microphone and put it back down on the table. Then she just stood there as if she was waiting for some reaction. None came. Everybody else was just standing there too. Eventually players began to shuffle toward their benches. They were followed by their now silent coaches.

— — — — — — —

The EMR team was not scheduled to play again for an hour. Coach Murdock herded them to a patch of bleachers at the end of the court. There she urged them to be quiet while she called AD Cardello. That done, she told the team that Mr. Cardello would be coming to see their next game, even though the varsity was playing at home.

"I'm embarrassed by having to make that call. I'm embarrassed to have jumped off the bench screaming. In all my years of coaching in places like Jersey City I never saw a riot like this one. Sandy, I know you were protecting Emily, but the way you did it was just not acceptable. Did my behavior cause that?"

Sandy answered, "Coach, I never saw what you did. This wasn't a riot. Where I come from both teams would have been out there swingin' at each other if something like that tackle happened. That bitch got what she had comin'. She was lucky I only got to hit her once."

Coach Murdock sighed. She remembered the old saw about taking the girl out of Chicago, but not being able to take the Chicago out of the girl. She said, "OK we'll be going small in the next two games. Emily will circulate between the low and high posts. We're going to need everybody to rebound without Sandy in there. Get hydrated and stay well away from anybody with West Morris colors.

The next game was against Randolph, a team that had whipped EMR by 16 during the regular season. Their best player was a girl of Emily's size who had beaten them soundly on the glass and in the post in their last game. Coach Murdock grabbed Emily and said, "You'll have your hands full in this game. No stupid fouls and don't try to do it all yourself. Your teammates can make the difference if you just break even with their big gun,"

Emily nodded, rubbed the bruise on her left elbow, and straightened the arm fully, testing it.

The game went as predicted. Emily figured that she might be able to run her opponent into the ground as the game went on. She kept rotating from the low to high post and back again. Sprinted out after getting a rebound and was rewarded with a couple of easy baskets when she got a step on her opponent. On the defensive end she attached herself to the girl's hip to make her constantly move. Caitlin was carrying the load offensively in the first half. The score was tied 23-23 at the half.

Coach said to Emily, "I see what you're trying to do. There are a couple of signs that it's working. Can you keep it up? I'll rest you a minute or two at the end of the third quarter."

"I'm good, Coach. If she stays in the game, I can keep going."

Gradually all those miles Emily had run during the summer and fall began to pay dividends. She burst past her opponent from the high post twice to score layups. The Randolph coach shifted a guard to double team Emily when she got the ball, and Emily was able to pass the ball to Caitlin, Nicky, or Jo for a good shot. She was also able to beat her worn-down opposite number to a couple of rebounds and cash those in. Randolph replaced their star with a shorter girl to give her a rest, and Emily had a field day in the low post on three consecutive trips down the floor. A time out did not disrupt her momentum, and about halfway through the fourth quarter EMR was ahead 54-30. Coach Murdock took Emily out to get some rest for the final game.

The Mt. Olive Gaels emerged as their opponent for the final game. They played a unique style, using ten players and substituting five fresh faces every four minutes. They ran like squirrels chasing a farmer with a leaking bag of acorns for the full 32 minutes of every game. They had run EMR off the court during the regular season.

Coach Murdock had done some preparation in practice since that debacle. They had worked very hard at a possession offense. The idea was to hold the ball until they could get an easy layup, and hope that Mt. Olive's racehorse style would lead to enough turnovers to let the tortoise beat the hare. In the days before the tournament Emily found she could fit into the slow- down offense quite comfortably. A key element of the strategy was to get the opening tap and score the first basket.

Emily was ready to jump center at the start of the game. "Throw it up high," she reminded the referee who was going to toss the ball.

"I always do," he replied.

And he did. Emily tipped the ball to the side, where Nicky grabbed it and lobbed it ahead to Caitlin, who was streaking for the basket in a set play. 2-0 EMR. Mt. Olive snatched the ball out of the basket and fired it to half court, from which a girl zipped to the basket to tie the score. Nicky passed the ball to Caitlin, who started to walk it up the court. She was immediately attacked by a double team. Emily burst into an open space at center court, and Caitlin passed her the ball just before the pincers closed. The defense dropped back. It had just been a fact-finding skirmish.

Caitlin got the ball back and stood in the front court far from the basket. The defense clustered around the arc and fronted Emily at the high post, waiting. A minute ran off the clock. Still nobody moved. Then another minute crept by. Jeers erupted from the crowd. Caitlin held her ground as instructed.

After another minute a Mt. Olive player started to rag on Caitlin. "Are you afraid to play? You're wimps. Your team sucks."

Coach Murdock addressed the nearest official. "That's taunting. That's a technical foul."

The official looked over at his supervisor who held his hand over his mouth. The official held up his hand facing the player doing the yelling and put his finger to his lips in the universal sign for quiet. At the same time the team coach was waving her hands back and forth across her chest. Her meaning was clear: cut it out. The crowd just got louder.

The standoff persisted, as if ten players were caught in a photograph. The defensive players looked to their coach for guidance. Caitlin just gritted her teeth and held fast.

With 15 seconds left in the first quarter, Coach Murdock yelled, "Go." Caitlin took two dribbles forward; the two defenders standing in front of Emily leaped to guard her; she bounced a pass between them to Emily; two more defenders closed on Emily, who passed the ball to Nicky at the side just outside the arc. Nicky took the shot. Emily rushed for the basket in case there was a rebound. Everybody else ran back on defense in case the Gaels got the ball with enough time to try to score. Nicky's shot went in with just three seconds left. The first period was over with EMR ahead 5-2.

At the start of the intermission the Mt. Olive coach ran part way across the court to yell at the referee supervisor. "Aren't there rules to prevent this? Don't they have to get past the hash mark or something?"

The supervisor yelled back. "Not anymore. If you want action, you'll have to go out and guard the player with the ball."

Emily said, "Coach this isn't basketball."

"Don't worry, things are about to change. They will press and trap.

They will grab and push you so you can't get available for the release pass. They may even foul like it's the end of the game to see if they can steal a throw-in pass or get us to miss a foul shot. Everybody needs to keep their cool and stay alert. Remember the only shots we're going to take are uncontested layups. Now, they get the throw-in to start the second quarter. We need to do our best to get a defensive stop and get the ball back. Then we'll see what they do. It may not be very exciting, but it's challenging."

EMR packed the lane on the throw-in by Mt. Olive. Eventually they attempted a three-point shot that missed. EMR got the long rebound and was immediately double teamed near the foul circle. Emily moved to be available for a pass, but found her shirt being held by a defender. Not much different from her AAU experience. She swatted the hand off her shirt and caught the release pass. Caitlin screamed, "Yo" as she sprinted down the court toward an untended basket. Emily threw a long pass toward her, and she made the layup.

Mt. Olive snatched the ball off the floor, made the throw-in, and raced toward their basket. They too made a layup, making the score 7-4, and pressed again. This time they double –teamed Josephine in a corner and forced a time out. Coach Murdock advised, "We can't spend a time out every time we get locked up. Keep the ball out of the corners. If worse comes to worst throw a long pass so that even if they intercept it, we'll have time to set up our D. Run our press breaks. Make them work!"

And they did make them work. When they got the ball to the front court, Mt. Olive went to a 1-3-1 zone defense, looking to trap in a corner. EMR kept the ball out of any corner, and patiently searched for a breakdown in the defense which might lead to a layup. Minutes passed with no scores. The crowd did not lose its voice. The Gaels did not have an opportunity to substitute, which took its toll on the defenders trying to catch EMR in a corner. Seconds before the first half ended, EMR forced up a shot which was unsuccessful. No one had ever seen a game like this. Still 7-4 at the half.

EMR had the throw-in to start the third quarter. Mt. Olive put their biggest player guarding the thrower-in in an attempt to cause an error. That did not happen. With the biggest girl trying to harass the thrower-in, the shorter defenders were at a disadvantage versus Emily. Caitlin was able to throw the pass high enough so that only Emily could reach it. She was fouled immediately, and the process was repeated. They again failed to steal the throw-in pass and went back to the zone defense.

The stress of taking perfect care of the ball and being alert for the slightest defensive maneuver began to wear on the EMR players. Sometimes the player with the ball was uncertain about whether she was subject to the five second count and got anxious to get the ball to a teammate. There was an occasional bobble on a pass, or an awkward dribble. Nerves were getting frayed. The Mt. Olive defenders lurked like foxes at a chicken farm waiting for their chance to pounce.

Finally, it happened. Nicky was closely guarded. She passed toward Caitlin just as Caitlin turned her back. The ball hit her on the rump and was snatched up by an alert defender. The girl raced for her goal with Emily in hot pursuit. Emily caught up to the girl just as she launched her layup. The whistle sounded; the shot went in. Emily was called for a foul.

The foul shot was good to tie the score at seven, and the press was on again. Coach Murdock got a time out to calm the troops. The Gaels got fresh legs into the game. There was one-minute left in the third quarter, and Mt. Olive would have the throw-in at the start of the fourth. The Mt. Olive crowd was beyond raucous, sensing blood. The EMR crowd just continued to hold its breath.

In the huddle Emily said, "We can run the endline on the throw-in. Get me the ball. If they foul me, do it again. If they double team, I can see over their guards to find who's free."

"OK," said Coach Murdock. "Use the out-of-bounds pass play."

But none of that was needed. Mt. Olive fell back to clog the lane on defense. There was no press. Nicky dribbled the ball into the front court and stopped. No one came out to guard her. The last minute of the quarter ran down. With 20 seconds left, Emily left her station at the high post and came out to the arc. "Gimme," she ordered, and Nicky threw her the ball.

Emily jumped high over the guard who came belatedly to contest her and launched a three point try, as she had been practicing with the JV. It swished through the net without even grazing the rim. There was stunned silence from everyone for a moment, then the EMR crowd erupted, and the horn to end the period sounded. The score was 10-7 in favor of EMR.

There was a lot of celebration at the bench, but Coach Murdock threw cold water on that immediately. "We have a long way to go, kiddies. This game is not over by a long shot. We have to get a stop and then fight like hell for eight minutes. They are going to be all over us like flies on roadkill."

Emily said, "Nothing has changed from before. Let's just keep doin' it."

"And remember we have three timeouts left," added their coach.

They didn't get the stop. Mt. Olive got the ball inbounds and ran a sophisticated double screen to get a layup. Then they pressed like demons. It seemed as if they had more than five players on the court, but the throw-in play worked fine, and Emily got the ball at the foul line. She was immediately double-teamed but found Josephine free and passed her the ball. Jo raced down the sideline into the offensive corner and was free for a long shot. However, Mt. Olive's biggest player was standing in the lane waiting to block any layup attempt, so Josephine dribbled back out behind the arc and passed to Caitlin.

Caitlin was doubled and passed to Nicky. Nicky was doubled and passed back. Caitlin got the ball to Emily at the high post, who was doubled by the big girl and a quick guard. She again passed the ball to an open Josephine. The national champion UConn woman's team could not hold the ball for eight minutes under this kind of pressure without a turnover. Coach Murdock asked for timeout.

"OK, guys, we're going to have to play basketball with them for the next six minutes or so. If we're still ahead then maybe we can put it in the deep freeze and make our foul shots. Regular zone offense, fast break when we can; take any good open shot. Emily you might get a turnaround shot from the high post."

Emily remembered getting stuffed doing that the summer, but this was a freshman game.

They made the throw-in deep into the backcourt and worked it into the front court against token pressure. Then the Mt. Olive 1-3-1 zone sprang into action, with their biggest girl the one under the basket. The way to attack that defense is from the corners, but you still have to get the ball there past the double teams to even start an attack. Emily moved to a space between two of the Gael's guards to receive a pass. She turned 90 degrees and passed to Caitlin who was free as a bird in three-point land in the corner. The big defender took a step toward her but stopped, confident that Caitlin would not shoot.

Caitlin shot. Emily raced for the open space the big girl had left. The shot was deflected down by the front rim into Emily's hands. She did not miss the put back.

Nor did she rest on her laurels. Mt. Olive got over their surprise quickly. They tried to throw the ball in quickly and race down the court as they had been hankering to do for the whole game. Emily jumped up and down in front of the player trying to make the throw-in, and managed to deflect the pass, giving time for her teammates to get back on defense.

The loyal group of EMR fans was roaring. Emily's father was standing in front of his usual seat, fist pumping in the air

Emily heard none of this; saw nothing of this. She saw only what was happening on the court but saw everything on the court. It was as if she knew what was about to happen before it did.

The Gaels moved into their high-speed half court weave offense. They used their biggest player to set screens around the top of the key. Emily was able to hedge out from behind the screen and prevent any three-point shots. She also boxed her opponent out to get the long rebounds and provide space for her teammates to get the short ones.

Emily scored no points during the next five minutes. Her teammates carried the ball. EMR was ahead by four points when the foul parade began as time began to run out. There had been few fouls in the game, so the Gaels had three fouls to give before the one and one penalty even applied. EMR managed to make all three throw-ins after the fouls successfully. The last one went to Emily with one minute left.

She tried to avoid being fouled, but a guard pushed her in the back. "That's intentional," shouted Coach Murdock. The referees ignored the plea to enforce the rarely enforced rule and awarded Emily a one and one. Emily smiled, made both shots and harassed the thrower-in.

The Gaels managed a score, cutting the EMR lead back to four. Emily broke away from her guard and leaped to catch the high throw-in pass. She was again fouled almost immediately. She smiled again, made the shots again, and harassed the thrower-in again. There were twenty-three seconds left in the game.

Mt Olive managed to make a three-point shot. As the ball went through the net the clock showed six seconds left. "Just leave it alone," shouted Coach Murdock.

A bewildered Caitlin picked the ball up and began to run along the endline trying to make the throw-in in the face of terrific Gael pressure. "No," yelled her coach again. "We don't have to throw it in."

She was right. The clock does not stop after a basket in a high school game unless someone is granted a time out. The final horn sounded while Caitlin held the ball. The strange game was finally over.

Everybody hugged everybody. Coach Murdock's conservative suit was a sodden mess after that, but she didn't seem to care. There was still plenty of fire in that mature spirit. After the handshakes and trophy presentation she cornered Emily before her parents could take her off.

"Emily, I owe you apologies and compliments. I was a little overwhelmed at having to deal with 16 kids on the freshman team. That was new for me. I was looking for simple ways to sort them out. Your missing the first day of practice was something it was easy to focus on. That was a terrible mistake, not because it hurt you in the long run, but because it was my failure to live my own values. I'm very sorry for that and very glad Coach Walsh had the courage to investigate.

"More important than that, I want to compliment you as a person." She waved to John and Janet to join them. "I think you should hear this too," she said when Emily's parents joined them. "Emily could have chosen not to play in this tournament either for the way I treated her at the start of the season, or because of her success on the JV. She would have been justified for either reason. She didn't do that. Rather she came to play with us, worked harder than anybody, and was totally unselfish. She is a marvelous young lady, and one of the most memorable students I have ever taught. Be very proud of her for who she is, not just for how well she plays."

Emily's eyes filled up and she and her coach hugged again.

John said, "Thank you, Coach. That means a lot.

Janet just grabbed Emily's sweaty body and held her close for a long minute. Emily rescued herself with a face that was puffed with emotion. "All right," she said. "Enough of this mushy stuff. We all just did what we were supposed to do."

John opened his mouth to say something but had the wits to close it again. He was learning more about his daughter every day.

CHAPTER FIFTEEN

On Monday all the JV girls and even some of the varsity team congratulated the freshmen on their win. The sentiment was returned to the varsity for their win in the state tournament on Saturday. They were to play in the next round on Tuesday, tomorrow. Emily hoped that the game would be in the evening. At the encouragement of her choir teacher, she was going to try out for the school chorus tomorrow afternoon.

Her choir teacher, Mrs. Turner, a short gray-haired lady who seemed as wide as she was tall and could blow the doors off a room with her powerful voice, had been enthusiastic about Emily's potential after several private lessons on proper breathing. She had said, "I've never had a student learn so quickly. You have a powerful voice. Next, we have to teach you to sight-read the choral music. One of these days you might be the star of the school's annual musical production."

Emily laughed at the time, but she did sign up for the chorus audition. Her only singing experience had been part time participation in her church youth choir. She liked to sing there, but often basketball had gotten in the way of going to church, and the choir shut down in summer due to multiple vacations. She had said, "I'm still in basketball mode, Mrs. Turner, and my father always says one thing at a time. I'll try out for the chorus, and then we'll see what happens."

"I'm sure you'll make the chorus," Mrs. Turner had answered.

So, there it was. Emily was committed to trying out once more to a competitive group. Today Mrs. Turner filled her in on all the requirements for the try out. Basically, she needed to decide what song she wanted to sing and bring the sheet music for the pianist who would accompany all candidates.

She had no sheet music for anything and no idea what to sing. *What the hell am I getting into?* she thought and went to consult with her mother Monday afternoon.

"Mom, last week Mrs. Turner talked me into signing up to audition for the chorus. The audition is tomorrow afternoon, and I have no idea what to sing. I found out today that I'm supposed to bring sheet music for the piano player."

"I'm glad you're interested in doing this," said her mother. "Can't you just sing one of the popular songs? You know the words to all of them."

"Yeah, Mom, but those singers have style. I'm no Adele and would look stupid trying to imitate someone like that."

"How about a standard? One that everyone knows how to play."

"Like what?"

Janet thought for moment, then said, "Can you sing *Amazing Grace?*"

"That's a hymn."

"It meets the criteria, and you've sung it before. Are you telling me they won't let you sing a hymn?"

"I don't know. Lots of professional singers have done it. I can't imagine anybody would get upset."

"Good. Decision made, unless you have a better idea."

"No. I guess I'll go up to my room and practice it a couple of times."

A couple of times turned into an hour, and Emily seemed satisfied with her progress when she came down for dinner.

———————

Of course, the piano player that accompanied all the singers knew Amazing Grace, so the first pass went smoothly. Just when Emily thought she was done the pianist said, "One more time," and cranked up the tempo. Emily kept up and found herself rocking to the beat. She liked it. It was fun. She liked to sing. Mrs. Turner applauded briefly when she finished.

At dinner Emily announced that her audition had been successful. She was now a member of the school chorus. Janet was delighted.

John said, "That's nice. What does the chorus do?"

"We sing at the assembly of the whole school that kicks off the student council elections, and we sing at graduation."

Her father suddenly sat up straight. "Isn't graduation on a Saturday?"

"Yes."

"That will get in the way of the AAU basketball tournaments."

Emily frowned. "I never thought of that. . . I guess I can miss one."

"There is only one graduation," said her mother.

"I meant one tournament."

"Whoa," said her father. "You'd be letting the rest of the team and Coach Booker down. You know how competitive those things are. You should be a starter this season."

Janet said, "We don't know that there will be a tournament the weekend of graduation. Besides that, we're only talking about Saturday, not the whole weekend."

John replied, "Last year June was very busy. They were getting ready for the trip to Pittsburgh. I doubt it will be different this year."

"Well, we'll worry about all that when Emily's on the team and we know the schedule." She stared her husband in the eye as she said this. He knew better to argue right then, but Emily knew that trouble was on the horizon.

As it turned out, the AAU schedule was not an immediate problem. The Morris Brown girls' team won its first-round game in the NJ state tournament. Coach Booker was busy scouting opponents and coaching at the tournament games. She didn't have time to get started on the AAU season.

Morris Brown played in what was called the "Non-Public" group against other prep and parochial schools. Schools like Pope John, Bergen Catholic, and Kent Place. Recruiting players was a non-issue in that section, because all the schools could do it. Some of these schools were better at it than others, however, and Morris Brown won its way to the state final in its group. The final would be played on March 20.

Emily kept one eye on Morris Brown's progress. Her priority though, was the progress of EMR's varsity in their section of the state tournament. They won two games, but got clobbered by Columbia, a perennial finalist in the group. Meanwhile, things started to heat up on the musical front.

The chorus was rehearsing twice a week for its assembly presentation. The director of the music department began inviting some of the singers to audition for parts in Cats, the musical the department would produce in the spring. Emily got invited to audition for the chorus line in the production. She knew nothing about dancing but found her athletic foot work provided a foundation for learning the few basic steps required and was awarded a part. She was one of two freshmen to be so honored. Serious rehearsals were to start in the middle of April.

Emily and her father went to the Rutgers Athletic Center to watch Morris Brown play in the state tournament final. She wanted to see how Ty and Jo did in their last high school game. It occurred to her that this might be the last time she saw them. They would be too old to play 16U in the spring. It was a close game and MB lost. Ty played hard under the boards but was matched by an equally large opponent inside. She managed nothing when more than 10 feet from the basket, while her opponent hit a couple of short jumpers. Those turned out to be the margin of victory. Emily appreciated once again Coach Simmons' demands that she learn to get and make shots 15 feet from the basket.

Morris Brown's head coach still looked as if he would have a heart attack, while Coach Booker was her usual calm and elegant self. Emily guessed that she would turn to her AAU duties soon.

Soon turned out to be the first week April. Coach B called Emily at home one evening. After the "how are yous" Coach B said, "I've assumed that you would want to play on our team again this year. Am I right?"

"Sure."

"You know that Ty and Ronna are too old for the team this year. We're going to need more height. The big girl on our JV is too old. Have you seen anyone who might fit the bill? We're getting a late start because of the tournament."

Emily was quiet for a moment while she ran images of the big girls she had played against through her mind. "There were several girls my size who were good, but nobody as big as Mo... There is the big girl who played on our freshman team, but she's slow and has a lot to learn."

Coach B laughed. "So, I can work my butt off training somebody this summer who'll help you kick our butts in the conference a couple of years from now. No thanks."

"Sorry."

"OK. I'm having tryouts this Saturday and getting the whole team together Thursday evening at seven. Are you good?"

"Thursday is good."

"Great. See you then."

Emily knew that the time to face up to schedule conflicts would soon arrive.

- - - - - -

John drove Emily over to Morris Brown Thursday night. He was eager to see what this year's team looked like. Mo, Rene, and Emily were the only returnees from last year's team. They greeted each other like long lost soldiers. When Mo hugged Emily she backed up surprised. "We can't call you Bones no more," she said. "We got to get you a new name."

"Emily is not too hard to say."

"Sorry, but that's wimpy. What else you got?"

"They called me Big E in eighth grade."

"I'm big. You're just middle-sized. How about just plain E?"

"Works for me," said Emily with a big smile. They pounded high fives.

There was no one among the new girls that even came close to Mo's size. There were several girls of Emily's size: one from the MB JV, another from Morris Catholic, and the star from the Randolph freshman who had played Emily head-to-head for most of the freshman tournament game. There were two very quick guards from Newark's 13th Street Tech. The rest of the squad was made up of girls Emily had played against in local JV match ups, whom she didn't remember much about. It was clear that Coach B's recruiting efforts had been hampered by the success of Morris Brown's varsity team in the state tournament.

Coach B's opening speech sounded grim. "We're going to have to run like mad and box out like gorillas if we're going to have any success this summer. We're going to have to press the whole game and steal some easy baskets. Everybody will get their chance in that effort. And we're going to have to be smart. Everybody will have to know what their role is and execute it every minute. It's going to take full commitment from all of us to win."

Emily felt a chill run down her spine. This kind of challenge always turned her on. Then she remembered that there may be a few games she would have to miss. Her soul twisted in that conflict. She would have to sort that out as soon as possible.

Mo wrapped her arm around E's shoulders after practice. She said, "Looks to me like it's gonna' be you and me carrying the team if we're gonna' win this summer. We got three water bugs for the back court, three rookies with some talent, and some fill-ins. It's gonna' be fun."

Mo left and Emily caught up with Coach B. Before she could say a word, Coach launched into her strategy for the season. "Emily, you're going to have to play bigger this year. Fortunately, you've gained 20 or 25 pounds and can jump out of the gym, but you're going to have to use that brain of yours to steal an advantage any way you can."

That made Emily feel even more guilty over what she was about to say. "Coach, I need the schedule for June as soon as you get it. I may have a couple of conflicts."

"What the hell are you talking about?" In her sneakers Coach B was a couple of inches shorter than Emily, but the fierceness of her gaze made Emily feel small.

"I've been selected for the chorus at school, and we have to sing at graduation. It's on a Saturday evening in June." She didn't dare mention the musical which would have its final performance the Saturday night a week before graduation.

Coach B's mouth dropped open. "A song fest is going to keep you from a basketball tournament? That doesn't compute."

Emily launched into the speech she and her mother had rehearsed for this moment. "Coach, I love basketball, but I'm not going to be six foot four. I may end up having a great career as a coach, like you, but there are some other things I need to explore. I. . ."

"Emily don't try to BS me," interrupted Coach B. "You're either on this team whole heartedly or you're not. Which is it going to be?"

"This team is in my blood, Coach. I was even rooting for Ty and Jo during the school season. Please work with me on this."

Coach B snorted and stalked out of the gym.

Where the hell does that leave me? Emily asked herself. *I guess it leaves me with another challenge to work out of.* She turned to go get her stuff. Her father was shrugging into his spring jacket.

"You look troubled," he said.

"Yeah, Coach B is mad at my singing at graduation. I don't know what she's going to do."

Her father stiffened. "Are you sure you want to be in the chorus?"

"Yes."

"Should I try to talk to her?"

Emily laughed, or maybe scoffed is the right word. She said, "Right now she'd bite your head off."

As they approached the exit from the building, Coach B stepped out of her office, and without a word, thrust a sheet of paper into Emily's hands. She immediately stomped back into the office.

It was the tournament schedule for the summer. Emily studied it on the ride home. The tournament on graduation weekend was a two-day event. Depending on the times of the Saturday games she might miss only one, assuming her father was a swift taxi driver. The tournament the week before would be a total loss because of the musical production. She folded the paper and put it into her backpack. She had some soul searching to do.

CHAPTER SIXTEEN

Emily lay on her bed on top of the comforter that night looking at the ceiling and thinking. Did she want to leave her teammates in the lurch to be in the school musical? Did she want to invest all the rehearsal time to be prepared for the production? How much interference with basketball practice or games could she tolerate? She enjoyed the singing. She doubted that she would become either a professional basketball player or singer, but both were where she loved to spend her energy at this point in her life. There was no easy way to do all of both opportunities currently on her plate. What to do? What to do? After a while she dozed off, still in her practice clothes. She dreamed.

Somehow, she was dressed funny: half of her had on basketball shorts and jersey; half had a full-length stocking with cat figures on it. Her arms were spread wide and a black woman in designer jeans and high heels, whose face was lined and had bags under her eyes, so she looked eighty years old pulled on her right arm, and a short fat woman with gray hair pulled on her left. The black woman was cursing. The short woman was singing "Jellicle Cats" Her body moved a few inches to the right and then back, as the woman on one side or the other increased her force. A big girl in a basketball uniform joined the woman pulling on her right arm. A man in coat and tie joined the singing woman, picking up the baritone part. Emily was crying, twisting her head from one side to the other as the stretch on her increased. Finally, she started to tear down the middle like a paper doll. She screamed.

Emily jerked erect on top of her bed, sweating as if she had just finished a game. In a few seconds she realized that it was a dream, but her conflicting thoughts were tearing her apart just the same. It was three o'clock in the morning and she had school today. She sat up on the edge of the bed, pulled off her gym clothes, and dropped them on the floor. She crawled under the cotton sheets in her sports bra and panties. Even though she could smell the fetid stink of the fearful sweat on her skin, she slept.

Janet had to roust her out of bed on Friday morning. "Are you OK? You look like you haven't slept."

Emily mumbled, "I'm OK." She looked at her clock and shouted, "Damn."

Her mother opened her mouth to protest, thought the better of it, and picked up the clothes on the floor.

Emily snatched clean underwear out of her drawer and ran into the bathroom in the hall. Her mother followed. When Emily looked into the mirror, she saw an ancient lady staring back at her. Tears welled. *How could she even go to school looking like this?*

Janet stood at the doorway and said, "Ems, get into the shower. I'll drive you to school. You can eat some breakfast in the car and feel a little more like yourself when you get there. Maybe whatever is bugging you won't seem so big then."

Some of the tension drained out of Emily. "Thanks, Mom." She reached for the faucet in the shower stall.

Janet was not about to waste the time alone with her daughter during the ride to the school. "OK, Ems, what's the problem?"

"I had a terrible dream last night. I was being pulled apart by Coach B and Mrs. Turner. Singing at graduation will make me miss a tournament game, and the musical will make me miss a whole weekend. The team is going to depend on me this year, but I enjoy the singing a lot. I don't know what to do."

Janet was quiet for two blocks, then she said, "It's a blessing to have more than one talent, Ems. Conflicts are part of life. We often must make hard choices. Remember all the fuss on Labor Day weekend? You can't play a game and sing at graduation at the same time. What are the options?"

They turned into the campus and started around the big circle that led to the front door. "I don't know about any options, Mom. Just let me off by the gym. That gives me the shortest run to my first class. I can just make it. Thanks. Maybe thinking about algebra will help me solve the problem."

Janet said, "Algebra can make you think. I'll think too. Have a good day."

Emily ran across the little bridge over the narrow creek that flowed in front of the gym and past the gym door to the path that led to the math class rooms.

She thought t*he techniques for solving algebra problems might help her work on her dilemma. X was peace for her in meeting what she saw as her obligations. It was clear that there was no way she could be in two places at the same time. What was the range of possible solutions which would approach closest to the desired value of X? What constraints could be removed to allow a path to that place? How could she quantify the relative importance of her obligations? Was my mother right that there are going to be many other hard choices in life? I really don't need that.*

- - - - - - -

When Emily returned from school she ran to her room and locked the door. There was no chance for her mother to talk to her. She called Caitlin and spilled her guts.

Caitlin listened, thought for a moment and then said, "You're kidding, right? Playing with that team got you to be a star on our JV this year and will sure get you on the varsity next season. You've invested a lot to get as good as you are. I'd give an arm and a leg to be able to play on your team. You can sing in the chorus next year when everybody at school knows who you are."

"I thought you'd say that."

Caitlin went on. "Look I know you want to do more than play hoops in high school. I know you want to please your mother too. You're different, Ems. You're special. So is your mother. She'll understand."

"I don't know, Cait, and then there's Mrs. Turner. She's helped me a lot."

"I haven't had any real big problems like this except for maybe conflict with Suzy over Billy. My mother is pretty religious. She tells me to pray when I'm stuck on something."

"That's something I haven't thought about. We'll see. Thanks." And then she ended the call.

After pondering Caitlin's thoughts for a while, she called Suzy.

Suzy was full of advice. "Emily, you'd be crazy to ditch the musical. All the good-looking guys in the school are in the cast. On top of that Tim Collins is in the chorus and he's on the basketball team. You'd be throwing away all those opportunities for great dates just to get all sweaty and smelly with a bunch of girls from the city."

Despite her angst, Emily had to laugh. "Thanks, Suzy. I never thought of that. I've got to go to dinner. See you tomorrow."

After repeated calls up the stairs Emily came down for dinner, her eyes red and face screwed into a scowl.

Janet put the bowl of mashed potatoes on the table and said, "Alright, out with it. What happened with your schedule problem?"

John asked, "What schedule problem?"

"The conflict between basketball and singing," answered Janet.

"Huh?"

"Yeah, Dad. I can't be in two places at the same time on graduation day or when the play is being produced."

"The team needs you a lot more than that big chorus would," he replied.

"The chorus is short-handed at graduation. All the seniors are busy graduating. That's why they hold auditions in the spring."

"But. . . ."

Janet jumped in. "Easy, John. Let's listen to what Ems has come up with. I assume you've talked to Caitlin and Suzy. Did they help?"

"Not really. I made a matrix like we were taught to do in Algebra. I tried to estimate how much pleasure I would get from doing each thing, and how much guilt I would feel if I blew it off. It took a lot of thought. I came to two conclusions: the musical is the loser; and I need to take a much longer view of possibilities before I commit to anything."

Janet said, "The musical is the loser?"

"Yes. Rehearsal doesn't start until next week, and there are others who want the part, so there was a very low guilt index for backing out. On the other hand, missing a whole weekend of hoops was a heavy-duty guilt trip."

John smiled. "What about the graduation?"

"Singing at graduation is on. Depending on the schedule I can play at least one, and maybe two, games on Saturday. Dad, I figured you would be happy to drive me from Montclair State to the ceremony. Coach B isn't going to be happy, but she wants to win. I'll have to sit some."

John's smile was gone. He opened his mouth to say something, but Janet cut him off. "Have you told anybody else about your decision?"

"Yeah, I talked to Mrs. Turner after school. She told me I had it wrong. It wasn't all about me. The chorus needed my voice and I had made a commitment to the musical. I told her that I understood what teamwork was, and then she got mad."

"What does that mean?" asked John.

Emily looked down at her feet. She almost whispered, "She reminded me that she had put in a lot of time after school teaching me how to breathe properly, and that she had supported me for a part in the play. She also said that school projects were much more important than outside recreational activities, and that if I wasn't loyal to the music program, I could just leave the chorus right now."

Emily burst out crying. Between sobs she shouted, "Why are people like that? Aren't teachers supposed to help us? I thought I had it figured out, but now I don't know what to do!"

There was a very long silence, broken only by Emily's sobs.

John said, "I never thought I would volunteer to talk to a teacher pleading for her to let you continue in an activity that would interfere with your playing an important basketball game, but I'll catch up with Mrs. Turner tomorrow morning and do just that. Maybe I can convince her that activities outside school are why kids do things in school and that basketball is important to the school too. Maybe I'll go see the principal."

Emily almost screamed, "Oh God no, Dad. I'd have to hide for a week."

Janet said, "John, this is my job. Mother to mother will be a lot more compatible than an irate father shouting at his daughter's teacher."

"I don't think Mrs. Turner has any kids," sighed Emily.

"Murphy never sleeps," snorted Janet. "I can see where she is emotionally involved in having you in the play, but if she throws you off the chorus, she'll never get a return on her investment in you. And I can fill her in on your investment in basketball and how you've contributed to the school program. I'm sure she's had other kids have to drop out of things. If she's fair, she'll agree she's better off with you in the chorus."

"And if she's not fair?" asked John.

"Then the principal is in for a conversation with an angry parent." Janet picked up the bowl of mashed potatoes and shoved it into the microwave. "Come on. I worked for an hour to cook this dinner and I'm not going to let it go to waste. Sit down and eat."

Janet drove Emily to school the next morning and set about her task.

After choir class that afternoon Mrs. Turner caught Emily's arm and, grim-faced, said, "After chorus practice this afternoon we'll go and see the music director so you can explain your decision to give up your spot in the play."

That was all she said, but it was enough to make Emily's day. The pent-up tension drained out of her, and she said, "Thanks."

— — — — — — —

Coach B said absolutely nothing to her at Thursday night's practice. The whole thing felt even more hostile when the coach played the girl from Randolph, Roberta, most of the time with the first string during the scrimmage. It didn't seem like a good time to force a confrontation with her.

Saturday's tournament was a one-day event at Queens College Prep again. The bus was leaving at 8:30 on a sunny morning. When Coach B saw Emily, she looked surprised. "What are you doing here?"

It was Emily's turn to be surprised. "Why wouldn't I be here?"

"I read in the Eagle on Thursday that you were in the cast of the school musical. The article went on at great length about how hard everybody was working to make it a success, with weekend practices etc."

Emily relaxed. "Coach, the article was wrong. I was originally in the cast but resigned when major conflicts with basketball showed up. The only conflict I will have might be a late game at the Montclair State tournament on Saturday, June 20. I told you about that already. Did you think that I wasn't going to be upfront with you?"

"I didn't want to, E, but the paper spooked me."

Coach B was silent for a full minute, then she said, "I confess I can get carried away coaching. I've been working at basketball since I was your age, and used that to get where I am. I don't have a lot of patience with dilettantes. Sorry I doubted you. Get on the bus. We'll worry about the state finals when the time comes."

They played hard at Queens College Prep and made their way into the final versus the home team. Mo and Emily had great games. They each scored fifteen points and had at least ten rebounds, but the rest of the team could not match their opponents' production. They lost 54-45.

As she made her way through the handshake line after the game, Emily saw the Prep head coach Burnside and AD Laughlin frowning at her. Each was probably unhappy for their own and different reasons. When she got to the end of the line, she saw the player she met a year ago, who was ticketed for Princeton, wave, and give her a smile and a thumbs up. *She hadn't included thoughts of vindication in her desire to show her ability to the coaches at Queens College Prep, but, though temporary, it felt good.*

John was at the game, of course. He wondered whether the frown on the coach's face meant that he realized that the diminutive former coach could still recognize scholarship talent and would have to be recognized in the future. John hoped so. Maybe he just rooted for underdogs.

■ ■ ■ ■ ■ ■ ■

The tournament at Montclair State the weekend of graduation was for the NJ State AAU 16U Championship. The Mauraders would have to win three games on Saturday to make the semifinals on Sunday. Thirty-two teams were entered in the random draw, with no team seeded.

Emily started the first game on the bench, punishment for her not being available for the late game. She wasn't worried about that. History said her turn would come.

And it did, sooner than anyone expected. Their opponent was an all-star team from Bergen County, big, fast, and coached by an assistant from the community college. They jumped to a six-point lead in the first five minutes and Coach B asked for time out. "E, come in for Roberta. Now listen. We're getting killed under the boards and not hustling back on D. That's got to change. If Rene penetrates, one of you other guards has to drop back to prevent their getting a chippie on a fast break. If you need to foul, foul. No more easy baskets! Now go play like I know you can."

With Mo and Emily alternating between the high and low posts and Rene hitting a couple of threes, the Mauraders crawled back into the game. Coach B rotated four players through the guard spots to keep the defense fresh. The gap was closed to two points by the end of the first quarter.

Bergen had the ball to start the second quarter, but Emily blocked a shot and set sail on a fast break. She received a nice lob pass and scored a layup to tie the game. A little of the air seemed to come out of the Bergen team's sails. The Mauraders kept the pressure on, Mo and Emily rebounded ferociously and fed the shooters. By half time the Mauraders were ahead by six. The second half was all theirs. Everybody got to play and get the competitive rust off.

The second game started just after one pm. It was against a team from Sparta that was as tall as the Mauraders on average, but not as quick. They played a zone defense which left holes in the middle and in the corners. Mo and Emily combined for 12 points and six assists in the first period to open a big lead by the end of the quarter.

About halfway through the second period, two Sparta players crashed into each other diving for a loose ball. One girl suffered a serious gash in her forehead and the other looked to be knocked unconscious. A long delay was required to get the para medics to the scene, bundle both girls into an ambulance to go to the hospital to be checked for a concussion, and to clean the blood off the floor properly.

The delay got everybody nervous. The parents of the players and their coach were totally distracted and worried. The tournament directors were struggling to revise the schedule, and Emily was looking at the clock. It was 2:15. She was due at her school by 4, and it was a 45-minute ride to get there. The game would take at least another half hour to play. It was going to be tight.

Maybe it was the long delay, or the memory of the sound of two heads crashing together, but the Mauraders let down in the third quarter. Coach B tried several combinations, but nothing clicked. Sparta inched back into the game. Mo couldn't seem to make a layup, and E was keeping one eye on the clock, so it was hard for her to score too. The Mauraders were ahead by four with two minutes left in the game, which had become a foul fest. Coach B asked for time out when they had a throw-in after being fouled. Emily was filled with a combination of anxiety and adrenaline. She burst into the middle of the timeout huddle and shouted, "This is crap. They're going to foul us, and all we have to do is make the shots. Gimme the damn ball and stay away. I'll take care of business and get the game over."

Coach B never said a word.

The inbounds pass went to Mo up high. She turned in the air and passed the ball to E before returning to the floor. Two Sparta players converged on E and almost tackled her. "That's intentional," shouted Coach B, but the referees ignored that.

Emily walked to the foul line deliberately, taking deep breaths and focusing her concentration. She had a one plus one bonus penalty. She stuck to her normal routine and made both shots. Mo jumped up and down in front of the girl making the throw-in causing her to delay. She managed to get a timeout just before the five second violation was about to be called.

Sparta ran a nice out-of-bounds play to complete the inbounds pass near mid court. They looked to make a long pass toward their basket.

Emily was lurking in the lane in anticipation of that. She intercepted the pass and moved toward open space. Sparta allowed her only a few steps before she was fouled again. Once more Emily made both foul shots and Mo harassed the thrower-in.

Frustrated, and with no timeouts left, the girl fired the ball into Mo's chest hoping to have it bounce out-of-bounds and get new throw-in. Mo stumbled back two steps, caught her foot, and sat down. Emily sprinted as if she were trying out for the Olympics to get to Mo before she could leap up. The last thing they needed would be for Mo to get thrown out of the tournament for fighting.

E got there in time. The ball had struck Mo's collar bone and bounced into her mouth causing her lip to bleed. Emily knelt in front of her with both hands on her shoulders. Mo swatted at them and tried to get to her knees. "I'm gonna swat the bitch. Get out of my way."

Emily held firm and locked eyes with her bigger teammate. "You can't do that, Mo. Remember last year? We need you."

"Come on, E. I can't let her get away with that."

"We'll file a hate crime lawsuit after the game," said Emily.

"Where the hell did you get that idea from?" Mo snapped, but the crisis was over. Coach B arrived and the two of them walked over to the bench where the school trainer was slipping on her latex gloves to deal with the bleeding.

Roberta came in for Mo.

There was a little more than one minute left in the game. "Keep the clock running as much as you can," ordered Coach B. They played hard defense but were careful not to foul. Sparta threw up a three-point shot that missed after twenty seconds. Roberta grabbed the rebound and passed it to Rene, who expected to get fouled. But Sparta backed off, their coach realizing that there was no hope and that tensions were about to explode.

After the final horn, the Sparta coach guided the girl who had thrown the ball at Mo over to apologize before the usual handshake line commenced. Mo didn't look happy, and her lip was swelling, but she didn't punch the girl either.

Meanwhile Emily was grabbing up her things and beckoning to her father. It was already 3:30! She waved at everybody, yelled, "We better be playing at noon tomorrow, you guys." Of course, if they didn't win at five today there would be no tomorrow. They hustled out of the gym and up the little hill to the parking lot.

"We have to go fast, Dad."

"Yeah, I know. I think I'll try the highways instead of the local streets. It should be faster."

Big mistake. Route 46 came to a screeching halt because of an accident just past the junction with Route 3. John inched along while Emily fidgeted. An ambulance roared by on the shoulder, convincing John that the road would not clear anytime soon. He looked around for any sign of the police. Seeing none, hoping they were busy with the accident, he drove onto the shoulder himself. In less than a mile he came to the exit for Ridge Rd. in a burg called Great Notch. He headed south.

"Ems," he said, "I think this road runs into 23. Can you check that on your phone?"

Emily scrounged around in her backpack to find the phone and open her GPS. "Yeah, Dad. Down around Cedar Grove they connect, then 23 turns into Prospect Ave. That will take us to 280."

"OK. Let's hope there are no more problems."

Emily looked at the time on her phone. It was almost four. She was supposed to be there looking good in the blouse and skirt she had folded neatly in the pack. The graduates were to be in their seats by five, and the Chorus would sing the National Anthem only minutes later.

Traffic on 23 kept moving, but at a slow end-of-the-workday pace. They were still a long way from 280 when they got caught at a traffic light at the Manor, a major restaurant with fancy grounds around it. Emily groaned to herself *We're never going to make it.* She threw her pack into the back seat, jumped out of the passenger door, and climbed into the back. John was too busy riding herd on his temper to even ask what she was going to do.

She grabbed some wet wipes from the container they kept back there and wiped some of the dried sweat off her face and arms. Next, she smoothed a few loose hairs back into her short ponytail, but the major problem had no easy solution. *She was not about to get naked in the back seat of the car. She could slip out of her smelly basketball uniform easily enough. That would leave her in her smelly underwear. The clean clothes would have to go on over a smelly body. Worse yet, the pretty blouse she liked so much would be going over her sports bra which made her look more flat-chested than she really was.*

Algebra could provide no solution to that problem. Fortunately, the graduation is outdoors so perhaps a breeze will blow some of her sweat stink away. Twisting and turning, wiggling, and pulling she removed the uniform and donned her clean blue skirt and white blouse. As her father screeched onto 280, she checked on her looks in his rear-view mirror. Her face was shiny, and she had no eye shadow, but it would have to do.

They arrived near the school at five minutes to five. Late-arriving family caused a major traffic jam starting two blocks short of the entrance to the campus. Emily grabbed her father's shoulder. "Turn at the next corner, Dad. The graduation is at the back of the school, and I can cut through somebody's back yard and get there quick."

John turned as directed. "Isn't there a fence around the school property?"

"Yeah, but there are holes. It's like this some mornings and kids can save a lot of time coming in through the back. I just have to find a big enough hole. You were really cool through all this mess, Dad. Thanks."

She blew him a kiss, climbed out of the car, and ran down the driveway of the first house into its back yard. John felt a nice warm glow run down his back.

The chorus was already in place on its risers when Emily sprinted into the large open green space in which the graduation was being held. The smell of freshly cut grass filled the air. Emily hoped it would cover up some of the foul odor she was sure billowed off her body. She hiked up her skirt a bit and rushed up the steps to her place in the third row of singers. Only when she got there did she remember that she would be standing next to Tim Collins, a cute, redheaded, very nice sophomore who had a few freckles across his nose, and who played on the varsity basketball team as well as singing in the chorus. She blushed, but he didn't seem to notice all the drawbacks she was so conscious of.

Mrs. Turner called up to her, "Welcome, Emily. Glad you could make it."

Everybody, including Tim, laughed. Maybe she was just trying to loosen the tension, or maybe she was giving Emily the needle in retaliation for all the trouble she had caused the music program the last few weeks. Emily took a deep breath and focused.

Tim asked, "How did your games go?"

Emily was shocked. "How do you know anything about that?"

"I was shooting some baskets with Billy Pedrazi the other day and he filled me in on your conflicts. How did you make out?"

"We won the first two. The rest of the guys are playing right now to see if we get to the semis tomorrow."

Mrs. Turner was tapping her baton on the lectern. Tim said, "Good luck. Looks like it's time to go to work," and took a deep breath prior to launching into voice.

All else went well. In addition to the National Anthem, the chorus sang a musical interlude later to break up the speeches. It was called "You are the new day". Emily thought it was a new day for her as well. She enjoyed singing with the group and the applause their performance merited from the spectators, forgetting entirely the trauma of getting there, and her appearance. She even forgot her self-consciousness about standing next to tall, handsome Tim. They high fived when they finished. It had been a great day.

Mo called after supper. "I told Coach B I'd call to save her the trouble. We won the last game, but she's not happy. Probably would have burned you a new one for not being with us. I didn't think it was that close, but they got it down to single digits twice in the fourth, so I guess that made her nervous. Anyway, we're playing the semis at noon. Don't be late. How did your singing go?"

"Great. We had a hell of a struggle getting there in time, and I'm sure I smelled like a dirty locker room, but nobody seemed to mind. I knew I could count on you guys to carry the ball. I'll be there bright and early tomorrow, all fired up."

"Get a good night's sleep. We have a tough one right off the bat."

"Will do, Mo. Thanks for calling."

When Emily came down for breakfast Sunday morning Janet was laughing at the photograph on the front page of the Morris County Record "Look, Ems. You guys made the front page."

Some photographer had decided that it would be a great idea to take a picture of the chorus singing the National Anthem. There she was, mouth open, sun glistening off her braces, her face shiny and without any makeup right on the front page of the paper. She thought that she looked as if she just wandered in from some homeless shelter in comparison to the other girls in the picture.

She whispered, "Oh my God."

Her father said, "We need to cut that out and stick it in the scrapbook, along with whatever we can find on the results of the tournament."

"Don't you dare," pleaded Emily. "I look terrible."

"You look like you're enjoying the singing," said her mother.

"I was, but look at my face compared to the other girls. And there I was standing next to Tim to top it off. Tear it up."

"No," said her father, "you and I know what it took to get you there, and I'm proud of how good you look."

"Oh, Dad."

Janet folded the paper and put it aside. "Pancakes sound good?"

"Always," replied Emily and John in unison.

CHAPTER SEVENTEEN

They were playing the team from Camden in the semifinal game. They were bigger than the Mauraders overall and very fast. As it turned out, they did not shoot well from outside. The Mauraders clogged up the middle with a tight zone defense, patiently waited for good shots when they got the ball, and won the game going away.

The finals drew a crowd of high school and college coaches. Some players were going into their junior year in high school and wanted to get on the college coaches' radar. Some of the high school coaches were there out of professional curiosity and/or off-season camaraderie; some were there to see what they might be facing the next winter. Coach Walsh came for that reason, as did the Morris Brown head coach, who looked as frazzled as ever even in shorts.

The Mauraders were playing a huge team from Flemington. Most of them played on the Hunterdon Central squads. Mo called then "amazons." She said to Emily, "I watched them play for a few minutes yesterday. We're gonna get bumped and thumped from start to finish. Make sure your bladder is empty."

Emily had laughed but took Mo's advice. Coach B started Jenna, the girl from Morris Brown's JV, to match up better size wise. Jenna was six feet tall, raw boned, and seemed to like to smack into people. As such she collected lots of fouls, but who knew how the game would be called today. There would be three officials, but none of them had demonstrated an interest in calling many fouls in either of the semifinal games.

The game turned into a bruising battle in the lane and on the boards. As the shortest of the Mauraders' "Bigs", Emily was getting posted up on the blocks almost every time the "amazons" came down the court.

Most of the time, she was playing a girl at least ten pounds heavier who kept trying to force her closer to the basket. Emily countered force with force, keeping her hands away and using her hip to meet the bigger girl's thrusts. The referees seemed to have no interest in penalizing either contestant. Jenna sometimes switched up with E but had collected two fouls early.

If Mo, Jenna, and E could manage the strength and stamina to neutralize the "amazon's" strength inside, the Mauraders' "water bugs" might be the difference in the game. Rene and her partners had a distinct speed advantage. Often, they could beat the other team down the court for a layup when Mo or E got a clean rebound and could make an outlet pass.

At half time they were ahead by six, but Jenna had four fouls and E could have spent the whole ten minutes counting her bruises. She had ten hard won points for her pains. Coach B inserted Roberta for Jenna.

Roberta wasn't strong enough to counter the size of their opponents, so the Mauraders went into a zone defense with Mo and E on the back line and the others dropping down to double team the ball when it got inside. Gradually their small lead began to trickle away. The "amazons" tied the score early in the fourth quarter. Coach B got a time out.

She said, "All right we have the ball and we're going to keep it until we get an uncontested layup. Am I clear? We take no shots except an uncontested layup. No crazy drives into a crowded lane, no open three pointers. We stand at half court with the ball under our arm if necessary. Is that clear?"

Emily said, "We did this in the freshman tournament. It drove everybody crazy, including us."

"Well, I hope it drives them to do something crazy so we can steal a couple of baskets."

Rene dribbled down the center of the court, loosely guarded by an opponent. She stopped ten feet over the division line. Her guard backed off another three feet. When nothing happened for thirty seconds or so, the guard moved up closer but not close enough for the referee to start a five second count. The guard looked at her coach, who was standing there with her hands on her hips. After a few more seconds she waved the guard forward. Rene was ready. She passed the ball to Roberta near the sideline, who was immediately double-teamed. Emily made herself available for a release pass and whipped the ball to the open guard in the corner. The big girl guarding Mo jumped out to guard her, and the guard passed to ball to Mo underneath. One uncontested layup in the bank.

The "amazons" came down the court and forced a pass into the low post. Emily got a hand on the ball knocking it loose. Rene pounced on it, started to fast break, but realized that she was outnumbered. She eased the ball up the court as she had before, but her guard played her much more closely this time.

Emily yelled, "Watch the trap!"

Sure enough, Renee's guard tried to force her toward the sideline where two of her teammates waited just in the front court. Emily moved forward but stayed in the backcourt. "Now," she yelled. Rene passed her the ball. She whipped it to Mo at the head of the key. The girl who contested the pass accidentally smacked Emily in the mouth as she followed through. Mo passed the ball to Roberta under the basket for another uncontested layup. It was just good execution of their standard press-break offense. The "amazons" asked for time out.

That was good because Emily's braces had torn up her lips when she got smacked. A thin stream of blood rolled down her chin and dripped onto her uniform. A referee noticed that and said, "You'll have to leave the game to clean your shirt and stop the bleeding."

Coach B was furious. "My player gets smashed in the face, you don't call a foul, and now you're going to make her leave the game in this crisis? That's . . . . .applesauce!"

The referee said, "Sorry we missed the foul, but she can't play while she's bleeding. It's the rule."

Meanwhile the Montclair State trainer had put on gloves and was wiping the blood off Emily's face and stuffing her mouth with cotton rolls to prevent more. That was done just as the timeout ended. When Emily returned to the floor the head referee said, "Whoa, you can't play with blood on your shirt."

Emily's mouth hurt like hell and her eyes were still watering from the blow. She screamed, holding the cotton with her left hand so it wouldn't fly into the official's face, "What! You're giving them the game!"

"I'm not going to listen to abuse. The rule is the rule", snapped the official.

Coach B arrived at that instant. "We want a timeout. We'll change her shirt."

The referee sighed in relief. "That works," she said, "but you gotta do it outside the gym."

Coach grabbed one of the girls who had not been in the game and said, "Your chance to contribute. Get out in the hall and change shirts with E. Fast!" they got it done while Coach gave the scorer Emily's new number.

In the last seconds of the timeout Coach B said, "We can look for a more organized press now, with one of their bigs guarding the basket. We're up four with three minutes left. We're faster than they are, but they're going to get those long arms into the passing lanes. We need to always be moving toward the ball. No lazy passes. No dribbling into traps. We have two timeouts left. They have the arrow. Take care of the ball and only uncontested layups. Be strong."

The "amazons" came down, got the ball inside, and took a short jump shot. The ball went in, and Emily was charged with a foul trying to block the shot. The four-point lead was suddenly one.

The "amazons" did press. The Mauraders were quick enough and practiced enough to get the ball into the front court without difficulty, where they held the ball, but had to pass it promptly because they were closely guarded. None of their options looked like an easy pass.

An "amazon" guard got a hand on the ball, and it bounced off Rene's foot. There was a huge scramble for the ball. The officials called a held ball. The throw-in went to the "amazons". Again, they worked the ball inside for a shot. Mo blocked it, but their opponent got the loose ball back. As the game clock entered the last minute, they took another short shot. It missed, but Mo fouled the shooter.

The girl made the first shot to tie the score. Coach B asked for their last time out. She said only one word, "Rebound."

The player missed the second foul shot. The ball was slapped around by many hands only to land in the hands of the foul shooter about ten feet from the basket. She took a jump shot. Emily leaped from near the basket and blocked the shot. It felt like retribution for how she had been treated in her first game the year before. The ball hit the floor and Rene was on it. There was no chance for a fast break.

Coach B yelled, "Just run the offense."

They did, but the guards were tough, and the referees were not giving them anything. As the clock ran down toward zero, they got the ball to Mo down on the block. Her guard was lying all over her back. Mo jabbed an elbow back into the guard's stomach to gain a couple of inches of separation and took a contested jump hook. The ball hit the backboard, then the far side of the rim and came off.

Emily slipped around her guard and leaped for the rebound. The ball came to rest in her right hand, and she pushed it back toward the hoop just before her arm was nearly torn off by a defender. She heard the whistle and the horn as she hit the floor and the cotton flew out of her mouth. Then she heard the screaming from her teammates. They dragged her to her feet and proceeded to beat her in celebration. Her rebound shot had gone in.

She got free of the melee and saw her father pumping his fist and roaring. She was surprised to see Billy and Tim standing next to him, yelling, and clapping. Suzy and Caitlin were there too. Even her mother was cheering as she ran forward, pulling out a handkerchief to wipe up the blood again dripping from Emily's mouth. Emily's whole body felt on fire. She flung her arms upward fists clenched, turned back toward the court, and leaped as high as she could. She was immediately sorry she did that as her fist hit the rim.

When all the celebrating and trophy giving was over and with her mouth again stuffed with cotton, Emily was slowly returning to the real world, Coach Walsh came to her and said, "We're not going to sneak up on anybody next season after this. You'll have the best defender from every opponent in your face every game. You better keep making your game better. I'll be counting on you."

Coach B appeared silently. "He's right about that. I'm already regretting what I taught you." But she said it with a smile, the kind only coaches proud of their pupils can share.

Coach Walsh said, "Thanks Coach. We'll have a donnybrook next winter."

"You can bet on that, big guy." They shook hands and parted.

As Emily left the gym with her parents, Tim and Billy intercepted them and pounded high-fives. She blushed when Tim said, "Maybe the three of us can shoot some baskets this summer."

Of course, her father was ecstatic all the way home, even though Suzy and Caitlin were riding with them. Her mother just sat and smiled. There was no traffic today, so the parade of praise couldn't last forever. Soon it became background noise like a TV blaring in the next room. Emily shrugged at her friends, felt relaxation overtake her, her mind, her body, her whole being. She was done; all her obligations completed; no new ones on the horizon; a chance to sleep in and get some sun at the pool, where she was sure Suzy and Caitlin had already staked out chairs on each side of wherever Billy chose to sit. She would demand a bikini this summer. Certainly, last year's one-piece suit would no longer fit.

Shooting baskets with Billy and Tim would be fun, but she was beginning to hope that she'd be able to spend some time with Tim somewhere away from a basketball court.

OTHER BOOKS BY BILL KENNEY

"Victims of the Past" (a detective novel)
"A Very Special Election" (same detective)
"Riding the Waves of Change" (a memoir)

Printed in the United States
by Baker & Taylor Publisher Services